**"If you are very, very good,"
she promised him archly,
"I will take you to
an enchanted place."**

"How good is very, very good?" he asked, pulling her near and nibbling on her earlobe. "I feel a real siege of bad coming on."

She sighed and tilted her head so that he could better explore the tender skin below her ear. "Good can be a relative term," she murmured. "The definition can change almost at whim."

His arms slid around her, brushing her soft breasts. "I'll be good," he whispered huskily. "You just wait and see how good I can be."

Dear Reader:

June 1983 marks SECOND CHANCE AT LOVE's second birthday—and we have good reason to celebrate! While romantic fiction has continued to grow, SECOND CHANCE AT LOVE has remained in the forefront as an innovative, top-selling romance series. In ever-increasing numbers you, the readers, continue to buy SECOND CHANCE AT LOVE, which you've come to know as the "butterfly books."

During the past two years we've received thousands of letters expressing your enthusiasm for SECOND CHANCE AT LOVE. In particular, many of you have asked: "What happens to the hero and heroine after they get married?"

As we attempted to answer that question, our thoughts led naturally to an exciting new concept—a line of romances based on married love. We're now proud to announce the creation of this new line, coming to you this fall, called TO HAVE AND TO HOLD.

There has never been a series of romances about marriage. As we did with SECOND CHANCE AT LOVE, we're breaking new ground, setting a new precedent. TO HAVE AND TO HOLD romances will be heartwarming, compelling love stories of marriages that remain exciting, adventurous, enriching and, above all, romantic. Each TO HAVE AND TO HOLD romance will bring you two people who love each other deeply. You'll see them struggle with challenges many married couples face. But no matter what happens, their love and commitment will see them through to a brighter future.

We're very enthusiastic about TO HAVE AND TO HOLD, and we hope you will be too. Watch for its arrival this fall. We will, of course, continue to publish six SECOND CHANCE AT LOVE romances every month in addition to our new series. We hope you'll read and enjoy them all!

Warm wishes,

Ellen Edwards

Ellen Edwards
SECOND CHANCE AT LOVE
The Berkley Publishing Group
200 Madison Avenue
New York, N.Y. 10016

Second Chance at Love

JADE TIDE
JENA HUNT

SECOND CHANCE AT LOVE BOOK

CHAPTER ONE

THAWN KNEW WHO he was the moment he appeared, long and lean as a racehorse, on the steps of the large trailer home. She pulled her pea jacket closer against the cold, sea-driven wind and turned away, pretending to study the raw cliff face beside her.

But she stared at the scarred surface blindly, still seeing the man walking toward her with all the suppressed energy of a coiled bullwhip powering his stride. Her heart began to pound a drumbeat against her ribs. He was coming out to see what she was doing on his property, and she was ready to tell him. But she hadn't realized before whom she'd been sent out to meet, and she needed a moment to recover from her surprise.

The permit application had said *Raphael Armstrong*. If she'd read the name aloud, she'd have realized it was *Rafe* Armstrong. She'd seen in the paper only a few days before that he'd completed production on his latest film.

1

Funny how she still couldn't resist reading about that glittery world she'd put behind her so vehemently.

It was a world she found difficult to ignore. Every time she opened a newspaper or turned on the television, there was a column or news spot about it. And now one of its leading members was bearing down on her as steadily as the ocean wind was chilling her to the bone.

By the time the scrunch of his Western boots on the crushed rocks was audible above the crashing of the surf, she was ready. She turned, purposely assuming an expression of impersonal efficiency.

"Mr. Armstrong?" she asked coolly, clutching her clipboard against her chest to avoid having to shake his hand.

But he had no interest in greeting her politely. His gray eyes were as cold as the overcast sky.

"You can get off my land right now," he ordered, his voice low and taut with menace. Despite the fact that she had every right to be there, Thawn felt a quiver of apprehension slide between her shoulder blades. "You reporters are like leeches," he went on, "always after blood. That may be considered part of the game when I'm working, but this is my home, and you're not welcome."

Oh brother, Thawn thought, almost amused. What an ego. She paused for a moment, running a quick glance over the muscular man before her, taking in the breadth of his shoulders beneath the off-white fisherman's sweater and the lean length of his legs in the well-worn jeans.

"I'm not a reporter," she said aloud. "Believe me, I haven't the slightest interest in your home or your private life."

The tension was only slightly relieved. His face lost its belligerence, but the smoky eyes were still watchful

and wary beneath the long, dark brown brows.

"You look familiar," he accused, as though that were something she ought to be ashamed of.

She shook her head, not replying directly.

"Then what do you want?" he asked shortly.

She tilted her head back, spilling honey-blond curls against her shoulders. "I believe you've applied for a permit to build on this land," she said slowly, not lowering her eyes though the sharpness of his steel-gray gaze might tempt her to avoid it. "You won't get that permit without an environmental impact report. I'm here to make one."

"Oh." He had the grace to attempt a conciliatory smile, but the warmth didn't quite reach his icy eyes. "I see. You work for Earth and Sea Resources, then. You must be the T. Carlton I was told to expect."

Nodding, she began to walk along the foot of the sea cliff. He followed a few paces behind her. She glanced up at the yellow and violet wildflowers that were spilling down from the soil above like tiny heralds of spring.

"From the plans you submitted to us, I infer that you hope to build right up on that rise," she said, raising her voice to be heard above the rhythmic roar of the surf smashing on the dark, jagged rocks of the shore. "Is that correct?"

"Hope?" There was a thread of amusement in his voice. "Are my plans really considered so feeble as that down at the planning office?"

She turned to look at him. His eyes were warm now, and he was regarding her with an expression that said he found her attractive. He'd decided she had no connection with show business or the press; therefore he could react to her as any man might to an attractive young woman.

He didn't recognize her at all. He didn't remember

the sumptuous parties they had both attended, he with a succession of lovely ladies, she with Mark Lund, a rising young assistant producer who looked upon Rafe Armstrong as his shining idol.

But that had been long ago, almost a year now. It had been another life, one she wanted to forget. Yet the thought of Mark still made her wince.

"Your plans won't be considered by Vista County at all unless they have a favorable environmental impact report attached," she countered, still cool and distant. The last thing she wanted to do was encourage Rafe Armstrong.

"That'll be mostly a formality, I should think," he said smoothly.

She quirked an inquiring eyebrow at him. "Hardly that," she murmured, turning to walk up the crumbling opening in the cliff face toward where he planned to build. The insufferable gall of the man, she fumed to herself. As a producer-director with a string of major and very successful films to his credit, he was used to getting his way with the people he worked with. He would find it was a different story here. This was the real world, not celluloid.

"The terrace will go right here."

She started as his hand curled about her upper arm, directing her slightly to the left. She hadn't realized he was standing so close behind her. "It will extend all around this side of the house. It's a perfect place to have evening meals in the summer."

Thawn stood on the make-believe terrace and looked out over the wind-tossed waves of the silver sea. The pewter sky served as a solemn canopy. Today the landscape was a study in gray and silver, but in summer it would more likely be blue.

The view would be spectacular. The lot was extensive and isolated, a piece of the California coast more than two hundred miles north of Los Angeles and two hundred miles south of San Francisco, along a stretch of land where there wasn't much private ownership. It was an area where only the lucky few could still attempt to build—only the lucky and the very wealthy.

Thawn glanced at the man beside her. His attention was also fixed on the sea, but as if he'd felt her gaze, he turned back to her and smiled.

She felt a strange sensation in her chest, a quiver, as if something had flipped over. It surprised her, and she widened her eyes for just an instant. Then she looked quickly away, but he must have seen her expression because his hand tightened on her arm.

She didn't know what was wrong with her. She never reacted so intensely to a man's casual touch and look. His smile had startled her, that was all. As she recalled the other times she'd seen him, she couldn't remember ever having seen him smile.

"The entrance to the house will be here," he went on, dropping her arm to walk over and kick a line in the dust with his boot. "With a huge skylight above the living room."

She wanted to tell him that the details of his architectural plans really didn't interest her, but she found herself watching him instead.

What was it about him that fascinated her? She'd noticed before how heads turned whenever he walked by, but she had always had difficulty pinpointing the reason.

He wasn't particularly handsome. His tall, slender form had a strength that didn't depend on bulky musculature, and his movements had a certain grace. There

was nothing the least bit effeminate about him, but he had a sureness of action, a confidence in aim, that made him nice to watch. His face was slightly long and just a bit angular, with piercing eyes and a wide, slashing mouth. His dark brown hair, thick and curling about his ears, was badly in need of cutting, and it formed a fitting frame for his striking gray eyes. Except for his eyes, there wasn't much about him that was special.

Yet he exuded a magnetism that was hard to resist. She watched him pace off the walls of the structure, not listening to what he was saying but examining him as though hoping to find his secret and thus be done with him.

"The study will be large, with doors opening onto the terrace."

Was that where he planned to screen his films for his friends? "Is there a special reason for such a large study?" she asked innocently. "Do you have something in mind for it?"

She could just see him snuggled up late at night with some gorgeous starlet on his lap, the projector going as he showed off his latest thriller or the new science fiction epic that was currently drawing record crowds. Show business people were all alike. She could do without them. "It looks big enough to be a theater, a special showroom," she commented.

He turned sharp eyes on her again, and for a brief instant she was afraid he'd recognized her. She would have to be more careful in the future.

Without answering her question, he walked over to stand very near her. She stepped backward, trying to put a little more distance between them.

"Are you sure we've never met before?" he asked softly. "There's something about you—"

"I'm going to be spending some time here for the next few days," she cut in hurriedly, gazing out over his land. "My job is to make a recommendation to the county as to whether your house can be built without detriment to the area, whether it will fit into the landscape, or provide a menace and an eyesore."

She glanced toward him. "I'll be going over the Geological Survey maps of this area, looking for faults, landslides, and other geologic features that might have bearing upon your building plans. I'll also be searching for evidence of animal and plant life that might be disturbed."

He narrowed his eyes, amusement glimmering behind the thick black lashes. "We don't want to scare any bunnies, do we?" he asked sarcastically.

She refused to smile at his joke. Didn't he understand that this was serious?

"Bunnies can take care of themselves. We want to ensure that no endangered species are threatened, that native California flora is not destroyed to make way for weeds."

He nodded slowly, his eyes missing nothing. "And just what are your qualifications for this job?" he asked. "What makes you an expert?"

She wondered what it would be like to be seeking employment with this man. From what she'd heard of him before, she knew he insisted on quality work. Now she could see that he would be particular and demanding, wanting proof and references for everything.

"I graduated from a reputable university in Iowa with a degree in environmental studies. My background includes plenty of geology and biology, as well as a bit of engineering. I spent two years as a teaching assistant, another four as a biologist with Los Angeles County. I've been working here along the coast for nine months."

Her eyes swept over him proudly. "I think I can handle this job, Mr. Armstrong."

He shot her a crooked smile. "I have no doubt about that." His gaze slid along the line of her cheek. "No doubt at all." Then his eyes met hers again. "But tell me, environmental lady, is there a nonbureaucratic name I can call you by?"

She wanted to say, "Miss Carlton, if you please," but she knew that would be a bit ridiculous. Instead she said crisply, "Thawn Carlton."

His gaze darkened. "Thawn Carlton." He rolled the sound of it over his tongue. "No, the name's not familiar. But that face . . ." He shook his head. "You're sure we've never met before?"

She looked up quickly. "I don't believe so. Now if you don't mind, I'd like to get on with this. . . ."

It wasn't an actual lie. No one had ever bothered to introduce her to him. Every party she and Mark had attended where she'd seen Rafe Armstrong had been a huge bash with hundreds of people. Mark had been so eager to get the great man's ear that he'd forgotten all about the woman trailing along behind him.

She remembered how Rafe would lean back in his chair like a king while the hopefuls—the Marks of that world—gathered around, adoration shining from their faces. If Rafe should deign to speak to one of them, single him or her out, it was like handing a rare jewel to a beggar.

"Did you hear what he said?" Mark would ask for days afterward. "He said he saw my documentary on public television. He said I seemed to have a flair for interpreting data dramatically.

"He also said the camera work was mediocre," she would remind him, but he wouldn't hear her.

"If I could just get him to look at that experimental piece I made in film school, he'd understand my use of symbolism to express multilayers of consciousness." Mark's eyes would shine with longing. "Then he'd see how in tune my methods are with his. I'd work as a gofer just to get a chance on one of his films."

Certainly with all that adulation oozing around him, Rafe had never bothered to notice a quiet woman waiting at the edges of the crowd.

No, they hadn't met before, not really.

And this meeting was lasting longer than necessary. Why didn't he go back to his trailer and let her get on with her work?

"I'll just tag along and watch if you don't mind," he said.

She did mind. She minded very much. But at least the speculative look had left his eyes. He hadn't remembered her.

There was no reason he should. Her face was hardly memorable, at least in her own mind. She was pretty enough, with a perky oval face, like an urchin's, and a snub nose to go with it. She knew she looked younger than her twenty-eight years, but she suspected her dark brown eyes came closer to revealing the truth. She felt within herself a new awareness and a trace of cynicism that she hadn't possessed before she'd met Mark, before she'd found out how much love could hurt. She was afraid it showed in her eyes.

A mantle of wavy golden hair floated about her in a breezy cloud, and she carried herself with the ease of someone at home in the outdoors. But there was nothing about her, she'd often thought, that could compete with the stunning starlets who poured into the film capital of the world. And Rafe Armstrong was a connoisseur of

the breed. Each woman she'd seen with him had been more striking than the last. No, there was no reason for him to remember her.

She didn't know why it was so important to her that he not make the connection between her and Mark Lund. Maybe it was because she'd sensed in him a reluctance to be "show business" here. More likely it was that she didn't want to remember herself. Those memories were the most painful she harbored.

She made her way through the low, seaside plants, filling her charts as she went, noting the composition of the vegetation, comparing the rock types she found to those shown in the Geological Survey map she carried, looking for clues to animal life.

Every detail found a place in her charts. Each piece of information was a part of the jigsaw puzzle she would put together to get a full picture of the lot.

Though she tried to keep her mind on her work, Mark's face swam before her eyes—his sunny, handsome face; his sparkling blue eyes: his curly blond hair. He'd looked more like a movie star than an assistant producer. And when he'd shown an interest in her, she'd felt on top of the world.

"Well, what do you think, Thawn Carlton?" Rafe's deep voice startled her, and she jumped guiltily, realizing that she'd been dreaming instead of paying attention to her job. "Am I going to pass?"

Deliberately she tapped the tip of her pencil against the clipboard. "It isn't you who must pass, Mr. Armstrong," she said firmly. "It's your plan of development."

"And?" he went on insistently, his eyes crinkling with amusement. "How does it look so far?"

Tilting her head back so that the sea breeze grazed her cheeks, she gazed out over his land. "There are quite

a few indications of trouble, Mr. Armstrong," she said smoothly. "Quite a few little rough spots we'll have to investigate."

He frowned. "Such as?" His voice was ominously quiet.

"Such as..." She turned to face him boldly. "Such as the access road to get onto your site. As far as I can see, it will have to be cut through that stand of cypress. The commission takes a very dim view of cutting down trees along this part of the coast."

He shrugged carelessly. "I'm sure we can come to some sort of an agreement about that."

"Perhaps. But there's also public access. What provisions have you made for access to your beach?"

His grin reminded her of the triumphant smirk of a wolf who'd just made his daily kill. "Providing public access has just been struck down by the courts, Miss Carlton," he retorted. "I do read the papers, you know."

She shook her head. "The law itself hasn't been struck down. The ruling only allowed exceptions to be made in individual cases, and precedent must be considered. If the public has had access in the past, you won't be allowed to close the area to them now. There's every reason to believe that you may have to provide access in the future."

His eyes had turned cold. "Let's leave that to the future, then," he purred.

She pointed up the slope from where they were standing. "Do you see that caved-in area? It looks to me like evidence of an ancient landslide. The question is, would the extensive cut and fill your plans would require unload the toe of the landslide, thus endangering your own house and the whole land surface from here down to the shore?"

He was standing closer to her now, looming tall and

masculine beside her. She had the distinct impression that he was trying to intimidate her. Nervously she assured herself that it wouldn't work. Clenching her long fingers into fists, she forced herself to continue.

"Then there's the problem of water. How far back will you have to drill to get sweet water? Do you have a permit for a well?"

No longer bothering to answer her, he looked down at her from an advantage of about nine inches, as though poised to begin countermeasures.

"Then there's visual pollution." Why was her mouth so dry? She could barely get the words out. "Building on a rise like that will be difficult to justify in the face of the commission's goals of encouraging all new development to blend into the landscape rather than produce raw, ugly scars on the land."

"Raw, ugly scars?" Startled, she realized that her words had shocked him. Indignation flashed across his face. "My house is going to be the most beautiful home you've ever seen, lady!"

"Oh, I'm sure it will be." She couldn't keep a trace of sarcasm from her voice.

It would be beautiful, all right. There was a wild drama to this land that reminded her of the setting of *Wuthering Heights*. Instead of moors, here there was sea, but the same raw emotions seemed to pulse deeply here, where ocean winds twisted ancient trees and swept against jagged cliffs, where white-foamed waves smashed their fury against the rocky shore.

It was a perfect setting for overwhelming passion.

Suddenly anger rose in Thawn as she thought of this lovely land being churned up by bulldozers just to build a hideaway for the love affairs of another rich, selfish man.

"Are you planning to live here?" she asked quietly. "Will this be your principal residence?"

His stare was curious. "Only time will tell," he answered suavely. Then he gazed out over the restless sea. "My profession involves pressures that are high and debilitating. I need a place like this where I can get away from . . . everything."

A nice little retreat where he could bring the latest starlet who was trying to buy her way into his pictures, somewhere the press wouldn't know about, a place where he could fulfill his appetites without considering responsibilities. . . .

Appetites and ambition were the two drives that pumped energy into the film world. The more she'd learned, the more appalled she'd been, until finally she'd known it was a world she couldn't live in.

"But just why do you need this house, Mr. Armstrong?" she persisted. "Don't you already have a house somewhere? Why must you take another bit of this precious coastline for your own personal use?"

His wide mouth was pulled straight and taut in annoyance. "I see," he growled harshly. "So it's a bit of bias I'll have to deal with, is it?"

"Bias has nothing to do with it," she argued, though she knew he had a point. "It's your land legally. But I do think you ought to consider the moral implications of what you decide to do with it."

She lifted her chin defiantly and met his steely gaze. "Meanwhile I'll be checking into the possible problems with your permit."

Suddenly his eyes were blazing with anger. Before she could defend herself, his strong hands were curled about her shoulders, lifting her almost off the rocky ground, his fingers digging painfully through the thick

cloth of her jacket. "I don't like threats, Miss Carlton," he rasped, his face so close to hers that his breath was like a hot flame against her cheek. "I don't respond well to them. You just remember that when you're working on my 'little rough spots.'"

She swallowed, fear slowing her thoughts and movements. But she still had her pride and courage. "All right, Mr. Armstrong," she managed to force out, "you have now proved that you're stronger than I am, that you can intimidate me physically. But that doesn't change anything."

For a moment she was terrified of him. She sensed his barely suppressed fury and was suddenly aware of her vulnerability.

Then, to her surprise, his anger evaporated all at once and amusement took its place. He threw back his dark head and laughed then set her away from him.

"You're a fighter, Thawn Carlton, and I like a good scrap now and then." He set her free. His eyes were crinkling with good humor, but there was still a spark of wariness in them. "Just as long as you fight fair," he added softly.

She looked up at him, shaken and struggling to hide it. She couldn't imagine fighting with him at all. If only she could leave right now and never see him again. Something in the current that flowed between them whenever their eyes met told her that Rafe Armstrong was just a bit more dangerous than she could handle.

"I always fight fair," she answered sharply, with more confidence than she felt.

The smile left his eyes, and he gazed down into her upturned face as though puzzled by what he saw there. She was suddenly sure he was about to touch her, to reach out and run a finger across her cheek, to take her

hair into his fist and pull her closer. Her breath came more quickly, and she watched, fascinated, while that intention flamed in his eyes. She stood rooted to the spot, unable to look away, unable to move, until the blazing look died and was gone.

He hadn't touched her at all, but she felt as though he had.

Abruptly she wheeled and started down the small canyon that opened from the cliff down toward the sandy shore, fleeing like a seabird from a mountain lion. Her heart was beating a wild tattoo against her ribs, and she knew her cheeks were flaming. This was crazy, insane. She had to get away from him.

But, of course, he was right behind her. Even as she welcomed the cold sea wind against her face and felt it cooling her raging blood, she heard his step. A wild panic rose in her throat. What would he do next?

"You'll be able to see the house plainly from the sea," he said casually from right behind her. "I like to think that sailors on passing ships will look at my house through their binoculars and feel a certain kinship with it."

Her back still to him, Thawn closed her eyes and drew a deep breath into her lungs. Nothing had happened. What was the matter with her? Nothing had happened at all, yet here she was behaving as though he'd made a serious pass. What a fool she was being!

"Why on earth should a sailor feel any sort of relationship to a house on the shore?" she asked, her voice slightly shaky but strong. She turned to face him for his answer.

He looked young suddenly, boyish, certainly less than the mid-thirties she knew him to be. He was obviously excited about the home he planned to build.

"Because this house is going to be different from any

other house around here. I had it designed to incorporate three things: the beauty of the rocky coastline, the Spanish history of the area, and the connection to the sea." He shook his head at her. "You'll see what I mean when you see the sketches. It's a stunning place. When it's finished—"

"You'll need your permit first," she interrupted meanly. "And that's what I'm here to see about."

She hoped he would take the hint and leave so she could get on with her work, but instead he grabbed her hand and began to pull her down the beach.

"Come on," he called above the sound of the wild wind and surf. "I'll show you."

Reluctant but unable to pull away, she followed him to an outcropping of rocks that spilled like children's toys from the cliff to form a tall pile in the water.

"Up here," he encouraged, dropping her hand, and beginning to scramble quickly up the rough surface of the rocks.

"What are we doing this for?" she asked as she followed, her feet slipping slightly, her hands catching at the cool, smooth surface of the larger rocks.

He laughed down at her. "Come on," he called. "Only a bit farther."

Thawn was a good climber. Under ordinary circumstances she would have had no problem with this easy trek. But her mind wasn't on what she was doing, and when the foot she was leaning all her weight on slipped, she began a slow, inexorable slide down the tumbled rocks.

She gasped and flailed her arms. Her clipboard went flying as she grasped for something to slow her fall. But the slope was covered with loose rock, and nothing was

secure enough to break her fall.

The larger boulders were just below her. She dug her heels in, trying to get some leverage, but it was no use. She was going to hit them.

She screamed. Rafe was below her in a flash, jumping from one rock to another. One moment she was staring down at the hard boulder that was sure to smash her silly. The next his arms were around her, breaking her slide, holding her tightly against him.

"Are you all right?" He studied her anxiously. She felt the flutter again, the melting turmoil in her chest that disturbed her unbearably.

Unable to speak, she nodded. He looked relieved, then glanced back up at their destination. "I wanted you to see the view," he began, then looked back down at her, still held close in his arms. A slow smile softened his features. "But never mind, this view is so much better," he murmured, and then his mouth was on hers, warm and comforting in the cold sea air.

She didn't resist. She wanted his kiss, wanted to feel the fire that his lips kindled in her. As his mouth tested her, working slowly, deliciously, to find her hidden sweetness, she responded as though to a lover, opening the way to his penetration, reacting to the challenge of his kiss with a demand of her own. Not allowing her thoughts to intrude, she let the feel of him flow through her in a bright golden stream of pleasure.

His hand came up to tangle in her hair, holding her so that she wouldn't try to escape. But she didn't want to get away.

When finally he drew back, his eyes were full of wary wonder, as though he was surprised by something she'd done. She felt her cheeks redden, this time with embar-

rassment. As he gazed at her speculatively, she recovered her poise, rising out of the pool of sensuality she'd allowed herself to swim in like a drowning woman out of a stormy sea.

CHAPTER TWO

CONFUSED, THAWN AVOIDED Rafe's eyes, and went to retrieve her fallen clipboard. She didn't know whether to be angry at his presumptuous embrace or to apologize for responding as she had. Both seemed a bit ridiculous under the circumstances, and she decided to try ignoring the incident.

But she couldn't ignore the way her blood was pulsing through her veins: neither could she pretend she hadn't enjoyed the kiss.

"There's not much usable light left," she said, gesturing toward the sun, which hung low in the late spring sky. She'd left this call until last on a busy day. "Only a couple of hours. I'd better get going here."

Rafe didn't answer her, though she could see his denim-clad legs from beneath her lowered lashes as she gathered the rest of her papers. She turned to face him, dreading what she might see, but his eyes were hooded and un-

19

readable, his face expressionless.

"Does my being along hinder your work?" he asked softly, watching her carefully.

She tried a casual laugh that came out false and strained. "As a matter of fact," she admitted, "I'm having some trouble concentrating. So if you wouldn't mind..."

He continued to stare at her. He was attracted to her; she knew that. Was he going to ask to see her again? She waited, pulse throbbing in her throat, not sure what she would answer.

But the question never came. Finally he seemed to draw himself up and away from her. "I'll be at the trailer if you want me for anything," he said crisply.

Without another glance, as though she were already dismissed from his mind, he strode off through the low chaparral.

She followed more slowly, wondering at the ridiculous flutter that still plagued her, the disappointment she felt now that he was actually leaving her.

She'd asked him to go, hadn't she? She'd wanted it with all her heart.

But no, that wasn't quite true. One small part of her seemed to wish very badly for him to stay.

He was so attractive. She wished she could put her finger on why. Then maybe she could fight his effect on her.

Stopping beside a cypress tree and leaning on the trunk that slanted away from the sea as though it was searching for an escape from the raw blast of cold ocean wind, she took another covert glance at the man who'd just turned her complacent world upside down. He looked so strong, for all his slender build, and he'd felt strong, too, catching her, holding her.

There was no denying her response. There was no

denying that she would like to feel that way again. They were bound to have more contact. Perhaps if they saw each other now and then while she was working on this report . . .

But as she watched it became clear why that could never be. Before he had even started up the steps to his trailer home, the door flew open and a woman stood framed there, welcoming him back. She was tall and willowy, with dark hair hanging over her face like a silken curtain. Thawn turned away quickly, disdain curling her lip.

Of course he had a woman here. What had she been thinking? And while the woman he'd brought with him for an idyll at the ocean shore waited for him in the trailer, he was within shouting distance, making a pass at Thawn.

Angrily she took out her mapping charts and began to try to work. She should have known. How could she have made that naive mistake again?

A sudden memory flashed into focus. Mark had taken her to a beach party at the Malibu home of a famous stand-up comedian. She'd enjoyed it more than any other party they'd attended together. They'd spent the afternoon chasing waves and walking along the sandy beach. Everyone had seemed free from the usual posturing, more real and warm.

Evening had fallen and the partygoers were straggling inside from the beach. Thawn stepped into the empty kitchen to get a drink of water. Around the corner in the breakfast nook, she caught a glimpse of Rafe Armstrong talking to a man she didn't know.

As she filled her glass, she heard their voices clearly.

"That's some beauty you've got with you today," the stranger was saying. "You have a reputation for dating

the best-looking women in town."

There was the suggestion of a smile in Rafe's voice as he answered quietly, "I do my best."

The other man's laugh sounded unpleasantly leering. "Well, I think you've outdone yourself this time. What's her name, anyway?"

Thawn replaced her glass carefully during the pause that followed and started to leave, but she heard Rafe's answer.

"You got me. I think it's Lisa or Tina or something like that."

"What the hell." The other man chortled. "With a face and body like that, she doesn't need a name."

Thawn had slammed the door behind her. It was a small show of temper, but she felt better afterward.

She'd quickly forgotten the incident, but as she thought of it now, she realized that Rafe was just like all the rest. Stories about his women had circulated through the industry. The joke went that although he was prolific as a producer, he made more unknown women into starlets than he did scripts into films. How could she have forgotten that?

With fierce determination she returned to her work. She would waste no more time on him.

Thawn walked carefully across the area on the rise where Rafe meant to build his dream house. Noticing the chalky whiteness of the strip where he'd dug up the earth with the heel of his boot, she moved closer and bent to examine the ground. Something about its appearance caught at her memory, and she took a small hammer from her pack and chipped away at the rocky soil.

A few inches down the chunks fell into her hand.

Curiously shaped, rounded and smooth, they looked familiar to her, though only bits and pieces of what they'd once been remained. Stealing another glance at the trailer to see if she was being observed, she pulled a sample bag out of her pocket and filled it with the specimens. Then she packed her belongings and walked purposefully toward her car. That dream house of Mr. Armstrong's just might be in more peril than he imagined.

"They're ammonites, aren't they?" she demanded impatiently later that night, picking up a piece and turning it slowly under the light. "Well, say something!"

Tom Sutton raised his blue eyes in mock disapproval and glared at her. "Science is not to be hurried," he drawled, purposely tormenting her.

She bit her lip and looked away in frustration. Tom was a good friend and fellow investigator at Earth and Sea Resources. He was also a trained paleontologist, and he loved nothing better than a good fossil find.

He raised the hand lens methodically to his eye again, and carefully examined another of the fragments Thawn had spilled before him from her sample bag. She made a face at the side of his woolly head, then sat down as quietly as she could, her tapping foot the only sign of her impatience.

Tom was as big and burly as a bear, with the temper of a grizzly and the cuddly qualities of a teddy. Thawn felt affection for him but no hint of physical attraction. They had dated a few times when she'd first moved to the area, and he had made several attempts to establish a closer relationship with her, but her calm yet determined refusal had finally convinced him that the most they could be to each other was good friends.

They were sitting now in the living room of Thawn's tiny beach house, under the light that hung over her table. The furnishings of the room were simple: chairs and couch covered with natural linen, a coffee table sliced from natural redwood and set upon driftwood branches; a bookcase covering one wall, holding her stereo and numerous mineral specimens, including one huge quartz crystal that glowed like fire when light hit it. Large, framed Audobon prints hung on the other walls, and plants brightened every corner. Thawn's interest in the natural world was obvious.

Finally Tom leaned back in his chair and smiled at her.

"Well?" she prompted. "What's the verdict?"

A wide grin wrinkled his broad, friendly face. "Ammonites it is. Some pretty good specimens, even if none is whole. Not a bad find for a rank amateur."

"I'm not a rank amateur," she protested, though she knew he was only teasing. "I may not have a master's degree in paleontology, Mr. Expert, but I've had enough geology to qualify as at least a knowledgeable professional."

"Sure you are," he baited her. "Quick, now, this is a quiz. Give me the period and era of the age of the dinosaurs."

"Dinosaurs were Mesozoic era, died out in the late Cretaceous period of that era about sixty three million years ago." She raised her chin in triumph, but he wasn't satisfied.

"Rise of the mammals," he shot back at her.

"Mammals were around in the Mesozoic also, but they really took off in the Cenozoic. Now Tom—"

"When was the first amphibian found?"

"Tom! Ammonites are not amphibians. They aren't

dinosaurs or mammals, either. And ammonites are what I want to talk about."

He shrugged his burly shoulders. "There's no point talking about the little devils. You're just going to have to take me to the site where you found them, first thing in the morning." He grinned. "Why don't I spend the night here so we can get an early start?"

She sighed in exasperation. He knew that game had run its course, but he couldn't resist tormenting her with it anyway. "Have you got your sleeping bag with you?" she asked pointedly.

"Sure do. Never go anywhere without it."

Thawn couldn't resist smiling back at his laughing blue eyes. He really was incorrigible.

"Good. Then you can sleep out on my porch. It does get pretty cold out there in the ocean air, but since you've got a down bag..."

He grimaced painfully. "The lady denies me her bed once more," he moaned. "She casts me out into the cold night, denying me the warmth and succor that only she can provide."

"Tom," she said rigidly, forcing herself to keep a straight face, "will you please get back to the point? How much importance should we attach to these ammonites? Will it be enough to stop development?"

Tom stretched slowly. "Can't say at this point," he said casually. "I'll have to take a look at the place myself." He picked up a piece of chalky white shell. "But I've got to admit, ammonite finds are unusual along this part of the coast. And if this one is as rich as you say, I think we've got a protected fossil site on our hands."

She nodded, staring down at the white pile before her. "That's what I thought," she said softly. Was that good news or bad? She was fairly certain her discovery was

going to affect Rafe Armstrong's intention to build his house by the sea. But try as she would, she couldn't take much joy in the thought.

"Ever heard of Rafe Armstrong?" she asked Tom.

He considered for a moment, then shook his head. "The name sounds slightly familiar, but I can't place it."

She smiled. Tom had no interest at all in movies. His whole life was wrapped up in the environment—how to protect it, how to interpret it. Compared to the wondrous monuments of nature, the things made by humans were so fragile and superficial that he had no time for them.

"Who is he?" Tom asked suddenly, and she looked up, startled out of her reverie.

"A film producer," she said evasively. "It's his land we're talking about."

Tom's gaze sharpened, and he leaned closer to her. "An old friend from Hollywood?" he probed.

"No." Thawn shook her head vehemently. "No, I didn't really know him in Hollywood." Though she rarely blushed, she felt crimson color creeping across her cheeks, branding her with its telltale flag.

She tried to think back over just how much she'd told Tom. He knew about Mark, though not his name. He knew about how she'd thought she loved him, how Mark had disappointed and hurt her. Tom considered it a lesson well learned.

"Stick to nature," he often growled. "The laws are clearly defined, and no one tries to use you."

He was looking at her now in a way that indicated his lack of belief in her disclaimer. She realized with amusement that he thought Rafe was the man who had broken her heart. She should explain that it wasn't so, but she really didn't want to go into it.

"Go home, Tom," she said, looking up with a quick

smile. "I'll pick you up in the morning on my way back up the coast."

He didn't move immediately, and she could tell that he wanted to stay. He searched her face, his brow furled with worry. "Is this the guy, Thawn?" he asked quietly.

She forced a bright laugh. "Whatever gave you that idea? Of course not."

He frowned. "If you want me to take over this job for you, I'll fix it up."

For just a moment she considered the tempting idea of letting Tom make the change with the high command, as they half-affectionately, half-indignantly called Dr. Pruitt, the managing director of the environmental consulting firm they both worked for. But she hadn't spent the last year toughening herself for nothing. She had to stay and see it through.

She reached out to give Tom's hand a firm squeeze before shaking her head and rising to hurry along his departure. "Thanks, Tom, but as I said, it isn't necessary."

But she knew Tom had seen her hesitation, and, protective bear that he was, he was ready to come to her aid. He stood but didn't move toward the door.

"That guy hurt you badly," he said softly, his eyes steady on her. "I remember what you were like when you first moved up here. You could hardly look a man in the eye."

She stood silently, staring down at her moccasin-clad feet.

Though he didn't touch her, his affection was evident in his fierce tone. "I won't let that happen to you again," he promised. "No matter what you say, I'm going to see that you're not hurt."

She stared at him in surprise. "Oh no, Tom," she

insisted, afraid her ambiguity had encouraged a dangerous misunderstanding. "It isn't the same man, honestly.
Don't do anything silly."

"Don't *you* do anything silly," he retorted gruffly.
With a final shake of his head, he stomped out the door
into the foggy night.

"See you in the morning," Thawn called. He waved
as he let himself into his battered old Volkswagen, then
backed out of her driveway. Thawn watched the head-
lights fade into balls of glowing fire in the thick fog.
Then the taillights, tiny pinpoints of red, disappeared
into the blackness.

Why couldn't she fall in love with someone like Tom
Sutton? A relationship with a man like him would probably lead to marriage, would provide the sort of warm,
loving companionship that could nurture a family. Wasn't
that what she'd always wanted?

She had let Tom walk away, but when she looked
into the brilliant blue eyes of a schemer like Mark or the
cold gray gaze of Rafe Armstrong, she was spinning off
into a rainbow, soaring through the clouds on a sunbeam.
The only trouble was, *they* had their feet planted quite
solidly on the ground.

With a deep sigh she turned back into her little house
and began to clear away the dirty glasses, taking them
to the sink to rinse. But in the silvery water that rushed
from the faucet she saw the blue-green depths of the pool
that lay like a shimmering jewel in the center courtyard
of the apartment building where Mark had lived.

When she'd first seen that pool and encountered the
exotic singles life-style that Mark's neighbors enjoyed,
she'd thought she had finally found the California of the
legends.

She had arrived from Iowa at the age of twenty-three,

still wide-eyed and naive. Getting a job with the county had been a lucky stroke, but the biological testing she was involved in took all her time and energy. Working weekends and evenings, she had found herself with less of a social life than she'd had back home.

Then excitement had flared. Gromeyer Studios asked for a consultant for a sequence involving dolphins they were filming for an adventure epic. The senior biologist who usually answered such requests was on vacation, and Thawn was chosen for the job. She drove out to Burbank, her heart in her throat.

The dolphins were well trained. She had no problem with the technical details. Still, the day passed in a whirl of confusion.

She felt very out of place among the grips, cameramen, and harried assistant directors, who always seemed to be asking her to get out of the way or to be quiet while the film was rolling. When a handsome young assistant to the assistant producer asked her to come with him for coffee, she gratefully followed him to the studio cafeteria. Her memories of Mark and the rest of that day were very vague. Too much had happened to her all at once. He had been only part of it.

But when he had called her a few days later and asked if she would like to grab a hamburger with him, she was flattered.

Thinking back now, she decided that her quietness had attracted him. She'd been a good listener. Every word that had come from Mark's lips had fascinated her.

She was sure he'd liked that. His ego had needed stroking at that time. Stuck in a relatively menial position, he had hungered for a chance to prove his worth. Having someone believe in him utterly must have been very satisfying. It was a faith hard to find in the com-

petitive atmosphere in which he worked.

They began to date regularly, and before Thawn knew it they were committed in a way that she was sure would lead to love and marriage.

She had assumed he felt the same way. And actually he might have. But his values didn't quite jibe with hers.

The Hollywood parties they attended were a thrill at first. In the beginning she and Mark seemed to be hanging on to each other for support, wandering about the carefully trimmed gardens and exquisitely decorated drawing rooms, their mouths agape at the sight of famous faces. But as Mark's talent began to be recognized, he gained more confidence, and eventually Thawn felt like a follower rather than a participant.

It was, "Hey, Fernando, loved your last picture," and "Listen, if they can get backing for a story about dancing gumdrops, these guys can swing anything..." while Thawn stood in the background, smiling whenever anyone looked her way, feeling totally inadequate.

She blamed herself. She knew she should push herself forward, take part in the conversations that ricocheted around her. But somehow she never could.

The scene seemed to move too quickly, like a merry-go-round that wouldn't slow down to let her aboard. Just when she thought she'd picked up on an idea she could comment on, the conversation would reverse gears and speed off in a new direction.

But through it all she had never lost the belief that Mark loved her. He told her so often enough. If he forgot she existed when they came near other people "in the business," well, that was her own fault. She would have to work on being more assertive.

At times she had suffered pangs of doubt. Long weeks

had passed when, involved in some project that consumed his every waking thought and action, Mark had seemed to vanish from her life.

But he was ambitious. She had understood that.

She could have understood it all, accepted it all, if only he had understood her.

Coming out of her reverie and throwing down the dishcloth she'd been using to dry glasses and plates, Thawn reached for her pea jacket, shrugged into the heavy coat, and headed outside into the swirling fog.

The air felt like a thick, wet blanket of gray wool, smothering the seaside community in a mysterious veil. Thawn walked across the asphalt street, then onto the cold, crunchy sand. She could hear the waves breaking on the sandy shore, but she couldn't see a thing.

Still it was comforting to walk alongside the huge, uncaring sea. Petty human emotions seemed so insignificant beside it. And what trouble they caused!

Against her will, her thoughts returned to the last Hollywood party she and Mark had attended together. Rafe had been there. So had Matty, a young scriptwriter who was a special friend of Mark's.

Thawn always had the uneasy feeling that Matty felt she, instead of Thawn, should be on Mark's arm. But though Mark respected Matty's thorough knowledge of the film world and enjoyed her company, he often denigrated her tomboyish looks and lack of physical grace. Matty knew as well as anyone that Mark felt no amorous inclinations toward her, and sometimes she expressed her resentment with venomous remarks directed at Thawn.

That evening was no exception. Mark had warned Thawn that he wouldn't have much time for her at the party. "Glenda Sayers is producing a sci-fi thriller that's

right up my alley," he told her as they stepped out of the Mercedes he couldn't really afford. "I can't risk getting any more than an arm's length away from her all evening."

"Do you really think you can win a job that way?" Thawn asked doubtfully.

Mark threw back his blond head and roared his amusement. "This is Hollywood, baby," he teased. "You gotta pay for what you want, one way or another."

You gotta pay for what you want. The phrase had reverberated through her for weeks afterward. But she had felt calm and unsuspecting as she walked expectantly into the gorgeous split-level home in Beverly Hills.

All the beautiful, talented, and desperately hopeful people had gathered together around a sparkling blue pool, soaking in the sun as they basked in the greater light of famous stars.

"Pimps and whores," Matty had whispered vindictively in Thawn's ear. "Nothing but a bunch of pimps and whores."

Thawn pulled away from the woman's clutching fingers, repelled by her cynicism.

"What's the matter, Matty?" she said caustically. Taking a guess at the reason for Matty's bitterness today, she asked, "Did they hire someone to rewrite your script for *Lost Angel?*"

The woman nodded, her short brown hair bobbing on her forehead. "You got it, baby. They said my stuff didn't have enough bite."

Thawn laughed shortly. "They obviously don't know how to mine your natural reserves, do they?"

Matty looked at her, surprised. "Hey, there just might be some fire in you yet," she said speculatively. Then

her green eyes narrowed. "But I wonder if you've got the guts to go out there and blow the whistle on lover-boy."

"Lover-boy?" Thawn had no idea what she was talking about.

Matty nodded, her eyes bright with malice, "You do know he's been sleeping with her every night this week, don't you?"

Suddenly Thawn realized she was talking about Mark. Her first impulse was to deny the accusations. She turned to look at Mark, who was sitting beside Glenda Sayers. The woman was a good ten years older than he was and slightly pudgy in her persimmon silk jump suit.

A smile curled her lips. "Come off it, Matty," she began. But before she could complete the statement, Glenda leaned toward Mark, her crimson lips parted and inviting. Mark smiled as he bent to complete the kiss. It lasted for a long, long time.

Thawn was shaking when she turned back to Matty, her eyes pleading for reassurance. "No," she whispered.

For once Matty seemed to feel some pity. Embarrassment swept over her hard features, and her voice was gruff when she spoke. "Don't take it so hard, you idiot. It happens all the time. He doesn't do it because he wants to but because he'd do anything to get a job on her picture."

Thawn stumbled into the house, searching blindly for a way out. In just moments her world had been shattered. Viewing that scene had forced her to face doubts that had been lurking in the back of her mind for months.

She walked down to Beverly Boulevard and hailed a cab back to her apartment. It was after midnight before Mark showed up.

He admitted everything readily. "It doesn't mean I don't love you," he assured her. "This has nothing to do with our relationship. It's strictly business."

He grew annoyed with her, unable to understand why his using sex to get a job on a film should bother her so much.

"Women have been doing it for centuries," he argued. "Every one of you uses your body to get all you can."

She stared at him as if at a stranger. How had she deceived herself for so long? She knew she didn't have any hope for happiness with this man.

Later, when she'd thought through the whole business, she'd realized Mark wasn't really such a bad sort. He had always been very good to her. He'd even loved her, in his fashion. The atmosphere of the film world was the poison, with its belief in living for today, of trying everything once, of doing anything you could to get that big break. In that environment sex became just another form of currency. And, as Mark always said, you gotta pay for what you want.

At that moment she had known she had to leave Hollywood. She had run just as fast as she could.

But, she admitted to herself ruefully now as she turned in the fog and headed back toward the dim glow cast by her porch light, she hadn't run quite fast enough.

Jacqui Blatts was a writer she'd met from time to time at parties. When the woman had shown up on her doorstep, claiming to have witnessed the scene between Mark and Glenda at the party and wanting to see what she could do to help, Thawn had been too full of agony to see through her act. She'd been only too glad for the shoulder to cry on. In no time she'd told Jacqui everything.

Only later, when she saw the scandal rag on the newsstand with the blaring headline PRODUCER GLENDA SAYERS SELLS IT LIKE IT IS, with a picture of Mark and Glenda kissing and Thawn's name quoted as a source, did she realize that the curious ethics of Hollywood had caught her once again.

At least the story had produced one good result, she told herself grimly as she opened the door to her cottage. Mark had stopped calling her, stopped begging her to come back.

In fact, he'd seemed almost beyond anger in his last call. He claimed she'd ruined his career. For a long time after that, his name had been absent from the show business gossip columns.

It still hurt to think of him. But Thawn hoped he hadn't been too badly wounded by the article. He had talent and deserved a chance.

You gotta pay for what you want. She'd paid, too. But she'd learned to stay away from show business people. Now if she could only make sure the lesson stuck.

Early the next morning Thawn picked up Tom and drove her little Fiat across the coast road, taking the hills and curves as though she knew them by heart. To her left was the ocean and the black, craggy rocks of the shore. To her right were rolling hills, with granite-faced mountains behind them. This was her favorite stretch of land, from Morro Bay to the south through San Simeon and Big Sur to Monterey at the north. This was where she'd found the peace to heal her wounds. And this was where Rafe Armstrong wanted to build his country hideaway.

She flashed a sure smile at Tom's sleepy face. "Up

late last night?" she asked, her voice teasing.

"Couldn't sleep," he agreed. "Unrequited love will do that to you."

A quick glance reassured her that he was smiling. She relaxed.

"There it is, just ahead," she warned him, then pulled off onto the dirt road that led to the Armstrong property.

There were no signs of activity at the trailer. The curtains were drawn at the windows, and Thawn wondered if Rafe and his friend were still in bed.

She averted her gaze, determined to ignore the trailer as she got out of her car. "The site is on that rise," she told Tom, pointing. They walked out onto the sloping hill.

Tom's eyes lit up at the sight of the extensive outcropping, and without another word he fell to work with his rock hammer and knife, carefully prying out chunks of the chalky substance.

Thawn watched him for a few minutes, but she knew he could work for hours without opening his mouth to do more than grunt in answer to her questions. Besides, she had plenty of her own work to do. Picking up her clipboard and the contour maps she'd brought along, she made her way down to the rocky shore to begin checking the mapping of the land there.

She worked for some time, attacking the cliff face with her rock hammer to study the mineral composition on a clean break, looking for signs of faulting or landslides, ancient or incipient, and checking the stability of the cliff. She compared these and other geologic features to those indicated on the contour maps. On the whole she found few indications of structural problems.

Thawn's work went smoothly. The cool breeze off

the sea invigorated her, and she began to wonder if Tom
had made a decision yet.

Leaning back on her heels, she brushed her golden
hair from her eyes, at the same time letting her gaze
sweep over the ocean, calm and shot with silver in the
early morning light. Suddenly a dark bobbing object
caught her eye. At first she thought it was a sea lion or
an otter, but as she watched it curiously, it came closer
to shore, and she realized it was a man.

She stood watching him emerge from the low, foamy
waves. Taking a deep breath, she tried to relax, to quiet
her raging pulse. But she knew it was no use. Rafe was
coming out of the sea, and the thought of seeing him
again sent the blood racing through her veins.

He wore a black skintight wet suit that was cut off at
the arms and legs, exposing his bare skin to the icy
waters, and now to the chilling air. His tan skin had
darkened further in the cold, and drops of water clung
to him, glistening like jewels on his elegantly muscular
body. Her gaze slid over his arms and along his naked
thighs, and she felt a tingle of response rising in her.

"Are you crazy?" she demanded as soon as he was
near enough to hear her over the crashing waves. "Swimming alone in this cold water?"

His grin was a slash of white in his dark face. He
shook his head, sending a shower of cold water from his
thick dark hair.

"I tell you what," he called back. "Next time I'll take
you with me."

He was close enough for her to see the pearls of water
that still clung to his spiky lashes, emphasizing his brilliant gaze.

"No you won't," she retorted. "I may go for a dip in

July or August, but I'm not insane enough to want to swim in ice water on a day like this."

Actually it was warm for an early spring day, and the sun was shining. Thawn had worn a light pink sweater, which outlined her slim figure, and her best-fitting jeans. Belatedly she wondered why she'd dressed so carefully. When Rafe's admiring gaze raked over her, she felt guiltily that she knew the answer.

"It's not so bad once you get used to it," he answered, but she could see that his thoughts were elsewhere.

"But what were you doing out there?" she asked, still unable to understand such foolhardy behavior.

"Exploring." His eyes lit up with teasing humor. "Getting to know my beach. Did you know there's a flat area out along the point?" He gestured toward the jagged rocks that spilled out into the sea like a giant's rock pile. "I'll bet seals use it when they're in the area."

He dug into the pocket of his wet suit. "Look what I found."

It was a rock the size of a golf ball, dark, lustrous green, and as smooth as soap.

"This looks like real jade," Thawn cried, delighted. "There used to be a lot of jade along the coast here, but you seldom find a piece as big as this anymore."

Rafe watched her with a slight smile. "Keep it," he said when she tried to hand it back to him.

"Oh, I couldn't." She was horrified.

"But I want you to," he said firmly. He would brook no argument, that was plain.

Flushing, she slipped it into her pocket, intending to have it appraised and polished before giving it back to him.

She looked up and caught his gaze on her, and once

again she was sunk in the warm confusion that he seemed adept at producing in her.

"I still don't know how you could enjoy swimming in such cold water," she ventured lamely, wishing he would look away.

The smile that quirked his wide mouth lent a flash of fire to his silver eyes, and she felt mesmerized by his gaze, compelled, like a swaying cobra before a flute, to move closer, ever closer, to his overwhelming presence.

"I guess the wet suit helps," she forced out awkwardly.

He nodded slowly, his eyes steady on her. "It does help in the water, but it starts to get awfully hot out here in the sun." With one deft tug he pulled down the huge zipper that ran from his throat to the bottom of his suit. The two sides of black neoprene curled open, revealing his bare chest and low-slung swimming trunks.

Her gaze slipped down the length of him. When her eyes came to rest on the dark hair that curled in circles around his flat navel, she couldn't seem to look away.

He was shrugging out of the suit, peeling it off his body like a butterfly emerging from a thick black cocoon. "Can you give me a hand?" he asked as the tight neoprene caught one of his arms at his back.

No! her mind shouted, but without thinking she reached out and tried to help tug off the uncooperative material. The skin of his back felt warm under her fingers. Water dripped from his wet hair to dot a design upon her arm, and her breath began to come faster, as though she'd been running very hard.

Clenching her fists around the wet suit, she gave a tremendous yank that expressed all her anger at the way her treacherous body was responding to his nearness.

"Ouch!" He pulled away from her. "Don't take my skin with it!"

But his eyes were crinkling with amusement. She glanced at his mouth, then quickly down at the papers she'd placed on a convenient rock.

She had to get away. He was just playing with her, knowing how she reacted to everything he did. She had to get away and keep away.

He was out of the suit now, standing before her in only his trunks. She steeled herself. "Don't you have a towel or something?" she snapped. "You're going to catch pneumonia."

His grin was cocksure. "All I need is a good woman to warm me up." He laughed, then reached out and pulled her to him as she'd been hoping, dreading.

She wanted his kiss more than she'd ever wanted anything in her life, yet she hated herself for her own desires. Fool, she chastised herself, stupid fool—even as she melted against him, turning her face toward him in anticipation.

He tasted clean and salty, and she loved the cool skin of his face against her cheek, the hot feel of his smooth flesh beneath her hands. His mouth was sultry temptation, and she felt deliciously weak.

CHAPTER THREE

"THAWN!"

Go away. Go away and leave us alone. Leave me here forever.

But the call had obviously surprised Rafe, and he jerked his head up.

Tom stood on the sea cliff ten feet above their heads. From the stern look on his face, Thawn knew what he was thinking.

"Friend of yours?" Rafe murmured.

"Yes." She removed herself slowly from his arms, noting with chagrin that she was trembling. Something in her hoped that Rafe would pull her back, curl her into his arms and challenge the world to try to pry her free. Instead his attention seemed to focus on Tom. "What's he doing here?" he asked evenly.

"I . . . I asked him to come along with me," she answered shakily.

His eyes returned to her, flashing silver fire. "What for? Protection?"

"No, of course not." But a tiny, wriggling voice of conscience disagreed. She knew that the thought of having Tom along when she faced Rafe had once seemed like a good idea. "I wanted his advice on something I found on your building site," she explained.

She had his full attention now, and he turned on her, every muscle taut with readiness. "And just what was it you found?" he demanded, his voice quiet, colorless.

"Ammonites." She leaned down to pick up her clipboard and papers.

"Ammonites?"

"Fossil shells of mollusks who lived millions of years ago."

He watched her for a moment, the muscle in his jaw working sporadically. "Fossil shells," he said with no emotion. "So what?"

She took a deep breath and looked down at the mixture of crushed shell and rock that they were standing on. "Why don't you come on up and take a look?" she suggested lightly, heading down the beach to the path that led back up to the rise.

"Tom, this is Rafe Armstrong," she said quickly, noting the look Rafe cast as she used the name he was famous for. Now he knew she recognized him. "Tom's a trained paleontologist."

The two men shook hands warily.

"Paleontology—that's the study of prehistoric life, isn't it?" Rafe said in a voice that almost accused.

"You got it," Tom replied evenly.

Rafe looked down at the chalky area that Tom had blocked off with string. "And what's this? Some rare

evidence that's going to clear up the riddles of the dawn of time?"

Tom grunted a positive response. "Ammonites." He picked up a handful and displayed the shell fragments for them both to see. "Quite a rich cache of them."

Rafe picked one up and rolled it between his thumb and forefinger, studying it as though he knew what he was seeing. Holding it up to the light, he stared at it for another long minute.

Thawn watched him, wishing she dared offer to get him her jacket from the car. He looked so cold, standing in the cool breeze wearing only that strip of cloth. She admired the way he stood, legs apart, body lean and muscular, like an athlete in his prime. She forced herself to look away.

He handed the fossil back to Tom. "Looks like any old shell to me," he said stiffly. "I could find you a dozen like it down in the waves right now."

Tom shook his head. "Oh no, you couldn't," he answered quietly. "These little buggers have been extinct for millions of years."

Rafe cast a disparaging glance down at the ground before them. "Personally," he ventured stonily, "they can stay extinct for all I care. What possible good can they do for anyone now?"

"Ammonites ruled the seas during part of the Mesozoic era. Some of these coiled shells were huge. Imagine a snail larger than a man." Tom's enthusiasm was irresistible to Thawn, but it seemed to leave Rafe cold. "Fossil finds like this are very useful for zonal correlations," Tom went on, his tone growing slightly belligerent. "Age dating of the strata. Geologic mapping of the area."

Rafe stared at him for what seemed like forever; then he grinned. "Great," he said carelessly. "Go ahead and age date. Go ahead and map. I'm going to get dressed."

He strode off to his trailer, the wet suit slung over one shoulder. Thawn noticed again the power he seemed to hold in reserve, carefully conserving what he used for every step. She wondered if the woman was still waiting for him. Maybe he'd sent her back to Hollywood. But she pushed that hope away. What did she care? He meant nothing to her.

She went back to work, though it was difficult to keep her mind on it now. As she moved about the landscape, she forgot all about her companion.

"You two certainly got awful friendly awful fast." Tom's voice, coming close behind, made her jump.

She turned to face him slowly, not knowing how to respond to his resentful accusation. For some reason she felt she owed him an explanation.

"It's just funny how these things happen sometimes," she tried, knowing how weak her statement was. "It's not anyone's fault. It just seems as if an action occurs that no one plans, a sort of accident..."

Tom snorted and bent down, returning to his work. "What I saw was no accident, Thawn," he said gruffly. "With a guy like him, it's second nature."

Thawn's hands suddenly felt very cold, and she rubbed them against her sweater.

"I just don't like to see you set yourself up to fall again," he went on, his head bowed over the chalky earth. "And with that sort of man, it's inevitable."

He was only saying what she'd been telling herself all along, but suddenly she felt she had to defend Rafe.

"How do you know that?" she protested hotly. "How

do you know what sort of man he is? You've just barely met him."

The look Tom threw her from beneath his shaggy hair was pained. "Come on, Thawn," he said softly, "I know what he did to you before—"

"You do not! This isn't the same man. What do I have to say to prove it to you?"

He shook his head and picked up a white shell, dropping it carefully into a paper bag on which he had written a full explanation of its source and preliminary classification.

"Has it ever occurred to you that maybe you let this sort of thing happen because you like it?" His voice was sharp, as though he were saying the words to hurt her.

Thawn turned to him in shock. "What on earth are you talking about?" she demanded.

"You." He rose and faced her, his mouth turned down in anger. "You, and the way you seem to be drawn to the kind of man who will walk all over you. What are you, some sort of masochist? Do you enjoy being hit on? Because you sure seem to ask for it."

She stared at him, furious. "Don't you dare speak to me like that!" she hissed at him. "What do you know about what I ask for? What gives you the right to insult me like this?"

She was ready to stamp off, but regret was already flooding his face.

"Thawn." He reached out and took her shoulders in his huge, bearlike hands. "I'm sorry. Really."

He pulled her close against his wide chest. The feeling was friendly and comforting, and she didn't draw away.

"It's just that I care about you, honey. And I wish there was something I could do to keep you from getting

hurt." He stroked her hair. "If I had the right, I would take you so far from that guy—"

A scrunching sound on the sand indicated Rafe's return, and they sprang guiltily apart. Immediately Thawn regretted it. There was certainly no reason they should feel embarrassed about their platonic embrace.

Rafe's eyes were dark and unreadable. He'd changed into black slacks and a crisp white shirt that looked like business attire. It was obvious he didn't plan to dig around in the dirt with them.

"Do you want to explain just what you're planning to do here?" he asked. To Thawn's relief, his question was directed to Tom. She was free to drift away to do her own work.

She wanted to stay out of earshot. She wanted to ignore Rafe Armstrong and return to the way things had been a day or so before, when he had been only a vague memory and a name that appeared regularly in the newspapers. But even while a part of her was absorbed in her work, her eyes seemed to turn of their own accord to gaze at him. Then she broke the point on her pencil and discovered that her only pen was out of ink. She headed back to the car for the supplies she kept there.

Walking swiftly, she detoured around the rise and strode through the clump of cypress that lined the little ravine along one side of the property. She'd almost reached the clearing again when a sudden flash of color caught her eye and she stopped, staring intently through the branches of the nearest tree.

A woman was walking through the grove from the other side. Though Thawn couldn't make out her features, she was sure it was the woman who'd greeted Rafe the day before at the trailer.

The woman saw Thawn at almost the same instant.

Thawn sensed her panic even at this distance, and in a moment, with a whirl of dark brown hair, the woman disappeared among the brush.

How strange, Thawn thought, narrowing her eyes and staring at the empty spot. Why would she be so shy?

But the probable reason came to mind quickly enough. Of course. She didn't want the world to know that she was hiding away with Rafe Armstrong. It was another version of the same old story.

Thawn mused upon the woman's identity. She didn't look much like the decorative beauties with whom Rafe usually caroused.

Maybe she was the star of his last picture. Or the wife of the star. Or the daughter of the major financial backer, someone with a place and dignity of her own, but also someone with a lot to lose if her sojourn here were to become public knowledge.

Thawn got a handful of pencils from the car and returned to her work site, trying not to look to see if Rafe was still with Tom. But out of the corner of her eye she could tell that her friend was all alone. She couldn't resist a quick glance at the trailer.

She'd actually stopped to stare at it, wondering if Rafe was inside, when his voice came from behind her. "You're looking in the wrong direction." His flat tone turned her to stone. "I'm right behind you."

She turned slowly, her face hot with angry embarrassment. "How do you know I was looking for you?" she challenged, but he ignored her question.

His eyes were as cold as tempered steel, and his jaw was set with determination. He wasted no time in getting right to the point.

"Are you going to restrain that boyfriend of yours," he shot at her, "or am I going to end up in court trying

to fight having my property declared a natural preserve?"

She licked her lips nervously. "A fossil site like this is rare for this area—" she began, but an ugly expletive torn from his lips stopped her.

"This land has been in my family since Spanish days," he said harshly. "I've been paying exorbitant taxes on it for years. And now that I finally have plans to use it, all of a sudden it's a national monument." He shook his head slowly. "I don't buy it, Thawn. And I won't sit still for it."

She returned his glare, hoping she didn't look as shaken by his anger as she felt. He tossed his hair back from his forehead in disgust.

"Play your little games if you must," he said tensely. "But just remember that I can play hardball with the best of them." He made a gesture as though to leave her. "I've got a business meeting in San Luis Obispo. We'll talk more about this later."

Not if she could help it. Not if she saw him coming. "Who's the woman in your trailer?"

Immediately she regretted her words.

He turned back quickly and stared at her eyes with fierce intensity. "What woman?" he asked softly, but it was an obvious stall.

She shrugged. "You know very well what woman. The one you brought up here to spend a cozy seaside encounter with."

Did her voice sound as vindictive to him as it did to her? Anyone listening would almost think she was jealous.

The fire that leaped in his eyes seared her nerves, but she held his gaze boldly. "That woman is no concern of yours." His voice was still soft, but with the softness of confident menace. She felt a chill in response.

"I was just wondering why she seemed so afraid of company."

His cheeks flushed with anger, and she felt herself backing away as though in fear of physical danger. "Leave her alone," he ordered harshly. "If either one of you bothers her..."

He stopped, glared once more, then started to turn away again.

"Wait a minute." What was the matter with her? Why couldn't she seem to let him leave?

"What is it?"

"I can't keep this." Reaching into her pocket, she pulled out the lump of jade and held it out to him. He stared at it for a long moment, then took it from her.

"What's the problem?" he asked tightly. "Afraid someone might consider it a bribe?"

Her brown eyes were wide as she gazed up into his dark face. "What did you consider it?"

His mouth twisted in mock amusement. "Only a very small down payment, surely."

Anger sparked through her. "Why do you assume that everyone has a price?" she demanded.

He shrugged his wide shoulders. "It's been my experience that everyone does."

Somewhere deep inside she realized that his cynicism was very close to her own, but she couldn't admit that right then. They weren't talking about other people. They were talking about her.

"I don't," she insisted stoutly. "Nothing you do will have any effect on the outcome of my report."

Then his hard hand was cradling her jaw and moving over the plane of her throat, the fingers slipping just beneath the soft neck of her sweater to trail a line of sensation along her collarbone. "What a shame," he mur-

mured, and the current that ran between them was almost a physical thing. Her eyes seemed to drown in his, and she knew she wanted him badly and that he desired her, despite the anger that raged between them.

Then he was gone, striding off toward the trailer. Thawn's skin tingled where his hand had touched her. She stood watching, and in a moment a metallic-silver Jaguar slid out from behind his mobile home, sending out a plume of dust as it roared off toward the highway.

CHAPTER FOUR

AT TIMES THAWN almost regretted her decision to live on the coast. As she sat one afternoon more than a month later, ensconsed in her cushioned window seat looking through the beveled panes of the tall window and over the gray sea, she felt twinges of that regret.

June had come and gone, and still the heavy coastal fog hung on. Inland, the temperatures must be soaring. She could close her eyes and imagine Fourth of July picnics, people lying in the sun, eating watermelons and spitting the seeds into their sprinklers while their children shrieked and splashed in swimming pools.

Meanwhile Thawn was still wearing sweaters until noon and searching in vain for the sun.

Her porch was her face to the world. Its cedar rails and rough floorboards had long ago turned gray in the cold, sea-driven winds, but she hadn't wanted to cover the natural effects of aging with decorative stain. Instead

she enhanced their beauty with hanging plants and pieces of driftwood dragged up from the shore. Creeping charley and wandering jew hung all around, a natural curtain between her and the outside world.

She rose and padded through the house, enjoying the swish of her full-sleeved caftan as it fell against her long legs. The deep purple color of the fabric seemed a proper echo for her mood, and she'd been putting off changing into something more practical for a necessary trip to the grocery store.

A mood of vague depression had her in thrall. Instinctively she felt that a good dose of sunshine would burn it away. She'd been a victim of it ever since she'd turned in her report on Rafe's plans to the county permit board.

The wheels of government tended to grind very slowly. It had been several weeks. Would the board turn him down?

She went over her decision again and again. Would she have made the same proposals if she hadn't known the owner of the land? Would she have cared about the ammonites if it hadn't been for Tom's urging to protect the area?

Yes, of course she would have. She knew that for sure. Yet there was something about the case that still disturbed her.

She'd returned to Rafe's property a number of times to complete her work, but she hadn't seen him again. Neither had she found any sign of the woman who was staying with him. Concluding that they had both gone back to Los Angeles, she'd felt a sense of relief mixed with uneasy disappointment.

Rafe had said they would talk again, and she had no doubt that if the verdict went against him, he would appear to discuss it.

She plopped down in her window seat once again. She really should go out and do some errands. It was Saturday, the only day she had to take care of the tasks that accrued during the week while she was working. But the seductive gloom of the sea seemed to hold her.

She noticed the soft purr of a sports car stopping on her street, but it wasn't until she heard the sound of footsteps on her porch that she snapped to attention. She waited, heart thumping, until hard knuckles rapped on her solid oak door.

It might be Tom, she told herself as she rose from the window seat. Or Lily, her middle-aged neighbor, who loved to chat over afternoon tea. But her pulse was racing as she turned the knob.

Deep down, she'd known it would be him. He was dressed in dark, snug-fitting pants and a white shirt open at the neck. His tousled hair and tan skin seemed even darker against the crisp cotton shirt.

As he faced her across the threshold, his eyes flashing with barely suppressed anger, she knew he'd had word from the board, and that the decision hadn't been to his liking.

"Hi," she said a little too heartily. "What can I do for you?"

He came toward her like a menacing storm, and she backed away quickly, giving him free access to her home. Turning, he closed the door carefully behind him. Somehow his restraint was even more alarming than a loud slam would have been. Thawn backed farther away until the back of her legs touched the table.

Rafe swung around to face her. "You did it to me," he said so softly that she could barely catch the snarling tone. "You and your scientific boyfriend stuck it to me good."

Thawn reached behind her, gripping the back of a chair. He seemed so tall, looming there before her. She felt threatened by his size. "We only told the truth," she answered breathlessly. "We only did our job."

She could see that he was having difficulty controlling his anger. "Is it your job to destroy dreams?" he rasped. "Is it your job to tear away the hopes of generations, just so the county ordinances will be satisfied? Just so that some crumbling old shells will be left to rot where they lie?"

"Is . . ." She wet her dry lips with her tongue. "Did they deny your permit?"

A ghastly grin containing no humor curved his wide mouth. "You know very well they denied it. You set them up to deny it."

"No." She shook her head quickly. "I only told them what I found."

"Did you, Thawn?" His voice was laced with sarcasm. "You didn't put a little emphasis here, a few adjectives there, that would have been better left out? You didn't guide the board members to the conclusion you wanted from them all along?"

His hard hand shot out and took her by the upper arm. "Are you telling me you didn't do any of those things, Thawn?"

His touch sparked her own anger. Who did he think he was, coming here to browbeat her this way?

"I certainly didn't mean to do anything of the sort," she retorted. "And if you think you're going to get me to confess by being physically abusive, you'd better reconsider."

He looked at where his fingers were cutting into her flesh as though he hadn't realized he was holding her. Quickly he withdrew his hand, but he didn't apologize.

Thawn's temper had been fueled now. She no longer feared him.

"You just can't take it, can you, Mr. Rafe Armstrong?" she mocked him. "You're so used to having everyone within earshot craning to see what your next desire might be that you can't accept the fact that there's a real world out here, a real world that doesn't give extra points for imaginative genius and Hollywood power. Here you have to follow the same rules as everyone else."

He looked surprised at her outburst, then slightly bemused. Encouraged, she raged on. "Maybe you ought to take a look around you, Mr. Big Shot. It might be a real education for you. There are other people in the world who make an even bigger contribution to the welfare of humanity than you do. They don't ask for special favors. What makes you think you deserve them?"

She stopped, more because she was running out of breath than because she didn't have more to say. But as she looked at him, something in his eyes told her that the cutting edge of his anger had been dulled.

"I'm not asking for special favors," he said quietly. "All I want to do is build on my own land."

A look of desolation in his face stopped the retort that was rising in her throat. His eyes reflected a deep, abiding suffering, and she felt suddenly astounded by the quality of pain she saw there. This wasn't the surface anger of a man who wasn't getting his way. This was something much more complex. Fascinated, she stared at him.

He ran a hand through his dark hair. "I don't think you really understand," he told her harshly. "I think you're the one who doesn't see reality."

She should throw him out. What right did he have to be there? She'd done a job on a government contract. His behavior now might be considered subverting the

proper channels, trying to influence her. He wasn't exactly offering a bribe or threatening her, but somehow this seemed just as wrong.

But she couldn't. Looking at him, she suddenly wanted to understand. She would never forgive herself if she didn't give him a chance to tell his side.

"Sit down," she told him quietly. "Let me get you something to drink."

At first she thought he would refuse, but his gaze wavered. "Okay," he answered shortly. "Have you got a beer?"

She walked quickly to the small refrigerator while he dropped into her largest chair.

When she returned with a tall, frosty glass full of golden, white-capped brew, she found him staring at the sea just as she had been only moments before.

He took the cold glass from her without looking up, took a long swallow, and leaned back as though letting the cool liquid restore his composure.

Thawn sat on the edge of her chair, watching him, noting how the grooves that lined his hard mouth were deeper than before. He looked tired.

"You must understand," she said again nervously, "that there was nothing personal in my recommendations to the board. I did what I felt I had to do."

The eyes he raised to hers were cold. "A picture of moral rectitude," he said softly, but there was no rancor in his tone, only sad bitterness.

She felt her cheeks reddening slightly. "I don't pretend to a higher righteousness," she protested, "but I can't neglect my duty."

"Your duty." He smiled thinly. "We're all in such a hurry to do our duty. How often do we stop to see where our duty encroaches upon the duty of another?"

She hadn't the slightest idea what he was talking about. "Why don't you tell me about your duty?" she tried.

His cold eyes were on her again. After studying her for a moment, his gaze slipped down and suddenly she was very aware of the low V-neck of her caftan. She straightened, and a smile twisted his mouth.

Raising his eyes, he finally said, "All right. Let me see if I can make you understand."

He put down his glass and leaned back in the chair again, his eyes searching the whitecaps out at sea.

"My great-great-grandfather, Michael Armstrong, came to California on that cold ocean in 1835," he said quietly. "He was a mate on a New England trader. He'd been at sea since his thirteenth birthday, when his parents died and he was apprenticed to a ship's captain. He'd never had any roots. But when he saw the Golden Land, he knew he'd found a home. He jumped ship, stayed to marry an *hija del país*—"

Rafe looked up at her with a slight smile. "That's a daughter of the land, a girl born and bred a Californian, who helped him adjust to the Spanish-Mexican culture that ruled at the time. Though he never earned the right to a major land grant to start a rancho, he was awarded a parcel of sea-swept land along the coast. He built his home there and raised his family."

Rafe moved restlessly, and Thawn had the impression that his penetrating eyes were looking back across the years.

"When the United States took over, he hung on to his land. Many didn't. But he'd lived in New England and understood deeds and the Anglo-Saxon legal processes better than most *Californios* did. Through the bad times and the good, he kept his land.

"His son was born there, my great-grandfather. And

then, as the century waned, his grandson, Gabriel Armstrong, was born there too.

"Most of the family was wiped out in one of the great influenza epidemics that killed thousands as the nineteenth century gave way to the twentieth. My grandfather, Gabriel Armstrong, was left alone. His mother, father, sisters and wife all died.

"Heartbroken, he left his seaside home and traveled south to Los Angeles in search of work. He found a job on the railroad. Eventually he married again—my grandmother. But he never lost his longing for the old life and the house by the sea."

The smile that tilted Rafe's lips matched the faraway look in his eyes. "When I was a little boy, he would tell me stories about the house and describe it—the red tiles, the roses clinging to the eaves, the Mexican rugs on the walls, the lanterns swinging in the fog. My childhood dreams were haunted by the ghosts of his memories."

He was silent, and Thawn watched him, touched by his vulnerability. Hearing this story of his family's past made him more real to her, more human. She almost felt she could reach out to him. Almost, but not quite. Finally she found the temerity to speak. "Didn't your grandfather ever go back?"

Rafe looked up as though surprised to see her there. "Yes," he admitted. "Once, when I was about seven, he borrowed my father's old Packard and drove up the coast to see the place. But when he came back to Los Angeles, he wouldn't tell me a thing about it. I never understood why until years later, when I came up to see for myself." He shook his head sadly. "There wasn't a trace of the house left. Hobos and other people must have carted it off brick by brick over the years. It was as though a whole lifetime had been erased."

Thawn murmured sympathetically, and Rafe turned the full force of his gaze on her once again.

"I want to bring that lifetime back, Thawn," he said earnestly. "It's too late for my grandfather—he died years ago. But it's not too late for the spirit of my family. I can keep it alive. You've got to let me have a chance."

His story had touched her. She felt his longing to restore his family's past, and she sympathized. But he was staring at her as though there were some magic wand she could wave that would make it all come right again. She gazed at him helplessly, turning her palms up in supplication.

"Rafe, there's really nothing I can do—" she began, then gasped as he lurched to his feet, his anger back in full force.

"Of course not," he spit out. "You've done it all already."

She winced at the bitterness of his tone. "Rafe, please..."

He swore softly. "I'm not going to stop here. I'm taking you and your boyfriend to court. We'll see what a judge thinks about your environmental crusade."

He strode toward the door, then swung back to glare at her once again. "I'm not sure why you did this to me, Thawn," he growled. "Maybe you really do think that your little white shells are more important than anything else." He shrugged his wide shoulders. "I think you're wrong, and I'm going to fight you all the way."

She made a movement toward him, but his eyes hardened in rejection. "I knew from the beginning that you were one of the crusaders," he said with a soft bite to his words. "But somehow I thought you'd at least be fair." He shook his head. "Those golden eyes of yours deceived me. They make you look like the last of the

real Girl Scouts—so wide, so vulnerable. I thought you were one of the most genuine women I'd ever met."

His laugh was a low, harsh sound. "You'd think someone with my experience in the contrasts between reality and illusion would know better by now."

He was out the door before she could say a word. She rose, her hand to her lips, wishing she knew what to say to clear the air, and explain her own position to him.

But wasn't that just what he'd been talking about? Hadn't he shown that he knew there were values more enduring than the momentary fame and the glitter of gold that he was so accustomed to? She knew now that there was more to Rafe Armstrong than the Hollywood producer. There was a man inside the image who had fears, pains and aspirations that had nothing to do with the stereotyped picture she'd had of him.

If only he would wait. If only they could talk...

She ran to the door, hoping to stop him before his car pulled away. But he was still standing on her porch, staring out at the churning ocean.

"Rafe," she called softly, and he whirled. "Don't go yet..."

She stepped toward him, reaching to take hold of his arm so that he couldn't escape. But suddenly she couldn't think of the words to make him understand. She stood staring up into his eyes, her hand on his arm, knowing her inner turmoil was clear on her face.

His eyes softened, then flickered with a new emotion she couldn't quite identify. The blaze of his rage seemed to blur with another flame, and then he was pulling her into his arms, his mouth covering hers with hard possession.

Anger had sharpened his embrace. There was a savage fierceness to his kiss, as though he meant to show her—

or himself—that it didn't cancel the enmity between them, that it was simply another aspect of it.

Thawn didn't struggle. Though her conscience told her that she must resist or lose her right to protest, her body was ignoring logic and inviting more of what Rafe offered.

His mouth was as smooth as silk and as hot as burning embers, and when his tongue forced open her lips, she felt as though she'd been invaded by a force of nature as irresistible as a flow of molten lava. It was sweeping her along, tossing her high in its menacing glow, carrying her into uncharted territory.

Thawn spread her hands across his chest, feeling the heat of his flesh beneath the cotton cloth. She'd meant to try to push him away, but when her fingers came in contact with his warmth, she found them curling against him instead.

Suddenly his anger was gone. Even Rafe had been seduced by the charge that caught fire and held between them. Thawn gasped against his open mouth as her legs began to tremble and she felt the thrust of his hips against hers.

At last he pulled away from her, but he brought her head against his chest, where she could feel his ragged breathing.

She let him hold her. She wasn't ready to meet his gaze, and it seemed safer to stay with her face against him, listening as his breathing became more even and her own racing heart slowed its pace.

"I came to declare war," he said softly into her hair. "I came to announce my battle plans." His arms tightened around her. "I guess this could be considered consorting with the enemy."

His words gave her the strength to face him. Pulling

away, she gazed earnestly into his eyes.

"I don't want to be your enemy, Rafe," she said quickly. "I listened to your reasons, and I think I learned a lot about you. But you haven't given me a chance to explain my side."

Slowly he unwound his arm from around her and let her drift away. His eyes held hers for a long moment. Then he nodded. "Okay," he said evenly. "Let's hear it."

Looking at him, she knew it was no good here. She'd never be able to make him understand just standing there on her front porch, staring at one another.

"Let's take a walk," she suggested, gesturing toward the windswept beach. "We can talk better there." She hesitated, looking down at her flowing caftan. "Why don't you wait for me down by the pier?" she said quickly. "I'll run in and change."

He nodded again but stood watching as she spun and fled into the house. Her heart was banging a drumlike crescendo against her ribs, but her instincts told her that Rafe was not unmoved by the electricity that snapped between them.

CHAPTER FIVE

THAWN SMILED AS she put on a persian melon lip color and drew her hair back into a slick pony tail after pulling on jeans and a bulky-knit tan sweater. She wouldn't think now. She would act purely on instinct.

She hurried out of the house and ran across the sand toward him, startling a group of large sea gulls that flapped into the air, protesting loudly.

He didn't smile as he watched her approach, but she could find no anger left in his face.

"Do you want to go out on the pier?" she asked. "The fishing boats are coming in."

He glanced at the small crowd gathering and shook his head. "No. Let's walk up the coast."

Thawn's house was one of the last buildings along that stretch of shore, and they were soon putting distance between themselves and civilization. Their feet sank into crusty sand still wet from the waves and decorated with

flourishes of seaweed left by the retreating tide.

A feeling of restraint had risen again like a wall to separate them. It was almost as if the kiss had never happened. Thawn glanced tentatively at Rafe to see if she could have mistaken his mood, but he was strolling beside her with his hands shoved deeply into the pockets of his jeans. He didn't look approachable, but when the sea breeze caught his nut-brown hair, her heart seemed to leap into her throat at the sight of him. She had to try to make him understand. Even if it was just for the moment, she wanted him to see that she wasn't the enemy.

"Have you ever seen the whales migrating through these waters?" she asked him quietly.

He shook his head in a curt negative.

"It's a fascinating sight. They swim north in the spring, south for Mexico in the winter. You can see them from the shore. They slap their huge tails down and blow water high into the air."

"I'm sure I'll have a wonderful view of them from my living room—once the house is built."

Thawn ran her tongue over dry lips. This wasn't going to be easy.

"In the old days the water was teeming with life— sea lions, whales, sea otters. Every one of them has now been threatened by man. The sea otters were almost extinct until they came under government protection."

Rafe whirled and stopped her with a hand on her arm. An angry muscle twitched near his jawline. "What are you trying to say, Thawn?" he demanded harshly. "Are you accusing me of wanting to kill off all the little animals?" He let go of her and gestured, palms open. "Do you see any blood on these hands, Thawn? Do you really

think my building the house will destroy Bambi and Flipper?"

Some impulse made her grasp his hands. "No . . . no!" He wasn't even trying to understand. "But don't you see? People are so adaptable. Most animals aren't. They must be protected or they'll perish and vanish from the earth, just like the ammonites did."

His strong fingers curled around her slender hands. "I'm not the big bad hunter, Thawn," he told her softly. "If there's a way to compromise, tell me. If we can save the fossils and still build my house, explain."

She'd always seen him as unfeeling, insensitive to the needs of others, but today she was learning that there was more to him than that. He was human. He had a right to his dreams and to his quest for something special.

"Are you really willing to compromise?" she asked tentatively. "If you could guarantee to keep the ammonite site just the way it is . . . if you redrew the plans for your house . . ."

"If we work on it together, I'm sure we can find a way."

She nodded happily. "We could try," she said hopefully.

A grin curved his mouth. "We'll do more than that," he promised. "We'll make a commitment right here and now. Are you ready?"

She smiled back. "All right," she agreed, not sure what he meant.

He raised his head and spoke to the sea and sky. "We, Thawn Carlton and Raphael Armstrong, do hereby pledge to find a way to build the house that will bring back to its rightful place the Armstrong family and protect the environment at the same time."

He cocked a shaggy eyebrow. "Is that official enough for you?" he teased. "Does an announcement to Neptune give it the badge of authority?" He lowered his face and smiled down at her. "But wait," he said softly. "We can do even better. We can seal it with a kiss."

His lips were warm and soft against hers. A blast of cold wind from the sea tore her hair free from its ribbon and whipped it about until it lashed both their faces.

"Come on," he said, his eyes alight with energy. "Let's explore."

Then they were running along the sand, her hand in his, searching for treasures among the piles of graying driftwood, hunting for gems among the surf-polished rocks, discovering tiny creatures in the tide pools. Thawn showed him how to catch sand crabs by waiting until a wave swept across the shore, then digging quickly down where a tiny bubble gave evidence of life and coming up with a wriggling little sea animal.

"They're cute," she insisted when he frowned and asked why anyone would want to catch them in the first place. "They feel so funny trying to dig down into your hand."

Rafe won the stone-skipping contest handily, but Thawn had an ace up her sleeve. "If you are very, very good," she promised him archly, "I will take you to an enchanted place."

"How good is very, very good?" he asked, pulling her near and nibbling on her earlobe. "I feel a real siege of bad coming on."

She sighed and tilted her head so that he could better explore the tender skin below her ear. "Good can be a relative term," she murmured. "The definition can change almost at whim."

His arms slid around her, brushing her soft breasts. "I'll be good," he whispered huskily. "You just wait and see how good I can be."

Then she was laughing and running from him again. The sun was peeking around the gray cloak that hid the sky, and from its low position, they could see that evening wasn't far away. But Thawn didn't care. She felt an incredible sense of joy. She hadn't felt so free or so happy in years. She knew it was a temporary sensation, but she didn't care.

"Here it is," she said in exaggerated whispers as she led him back away from the sea, along the sides of a small creek that ran down from the distant mountains. "You must go quietly so as not to break the spell."

"You must go quietly," Rafe corrected as he stepped over a bent piece of barbed-wire fencing, "so as not to alert the farmer through whose field we are trespassing."

She threw him a look of outrage. "How did you ever get into movie making with such a lack of imagination?" she accused. "You'd better be quiet or the bad sea witch will hear you and turn you into a toad. Her spells can be difficult to break."

He caught her by the neck and pulled her back for a quick, hungry kiss. "When do I get to sample one of your spells?" he asked, his eyelids heavy with sensual provocation. "I want to see exactly what you turn me into."

Her blood raced with excitement, fully aware of what he was suggesting. Was she brave enough to risk that again?

"Isn't it magnificent?" She turned to draw him into the circle of her radiant smile, giving it all to him—the crystal-clear pond with its round lily pads and shiny green

frogs, the fragrance of flowers blooming, the soft buzzing of bees, and the huge, spiny sprays hanging heavy with wild blackberries.

He grinned at her. She could see that he wasn't quite as enchanted by the setting as she might have liked, but willing to like it if she did. "Just the place for a newly formed toad," he said dryly.

"Don't worry," she consoled him. "If she does turn you into a toad, I'll kiss you quick and get back my handsome prince."

"Why don't you kiss me quick anyway?" he murmured against her neck, and she turned willingly in his arms and did just that.

They broke away breathlessly and hurried to gather and eat blackberries, until their fingers were stained, and then they teased frogs just to hear them splash into the warm water.

"What will the sea witch turn you into?" Rafe asked curiously at one point, when Thawn had been laughing loudly enough to threaten the spell.

"A dragonfly," she answered promptly. "A huge, electric-blue dragonfly with lacy wings."

He grinned wolfishly. "One perfect meal for a toad."

They were resting in a grassy hollow between high blackberry bushes and a thicket of thistles. Rafe lay back lazily, his head in Thawn's blue-jeaned lap, while she popped the swollen purple berries into his open mouth.

"Does the farmer—" he began.

"Sea witch," she corrected him hurriedly.

He smiled. "Does the sea witch ever make an appearance here?"

She nodded. "The sea witch has been known to watch from yonder hill with binoculars," she admitted. "That's what makes our journey here so deliciously dangerous."

Slowly he reached up and softly cupped her breast with his large hand. His eyes were clouded with intent when he spoke again. "What we need now is an enchanted sea cave."

Thawn hesitated. Should she tell him? She knew what she was inviting if she did. "I know of one," she said softly, before she could reconsider.

He sat up slowly, holding her gaze. "Do you?" he said gently. "Where is it?"

"I'll take you there," she said, her eyes burning into his.

In moments they found the rounded caves cut into the sandstone by ancient waves. Thawn had been there once months before, when Tom's ten-year-old cousin had shown them to her as a secret she must never tell.

"You have to get down on your hands and knees to enter," she told Rafe, cursing the tremor in her voice. "But inside you can stand up."

From the outside no one would dream such spacious rooms existed along the shoreline. The relentless sea had smoothed the sides and carved blowholes along the ceiling, which now let in the late afternoon light. The sand beneath their feet was as soft as velvet. The air was cool, but protected from the ocean breezes, the temperature was not unpleasant.

"Maybe I'll just move in here," Rafe said admiringly, looking around. "I don't imagine I'd need much of a permit, do you?"

She shook her head without answering, then reached out to touch the smooth cave walls. Rafe came up behind her, his hands sliding under her sweater to cup her breasts.

"Do I need a permit to make love to you, Thawn?" he whispered against her ear. "Do we need to chart the impact first?"

Her breath was coming quickly. Was she really so afraid? Perhaps she did need to stop and think about what making love with Rafe would cost her. But she didn't want to. She wouldn't.

"I think the impact will be self-explanatory," she murmured back, twisting in his arms until she faced him. "Permit granted," she whispered shakily.

But he didn't sweep her into an embrace as she expected. Instead he looked quietly down at her.

"I've wanted you since the moment you fell into my arms on my sea cliff," he told her huskily. A bittersweet smile tugged at the corners of his lips. "With your freckled nose and wide, innocent eyes, I knew loving you would be something special."

He dropped soft, exploratory kisses along her lips, across the bridge of her nose, and over her lowered eyelids.

"You're so different from the women I'm used to," he murmured, almost more to himself than to her. "So real and natural." He tilted her face up to receive him, and then his tongue mastered her mouth, entering to take possession like a pirate boarding a captive ship.

She kissed him back with no regrets. She wanted this as much as he did.

His hands moved down and slipped beneath her sweater again, this time to work their way into the smooth skin at the small of her back. He quickly found the gap where her jeans didn't quite hug her body, and his warm hands plunged down to knead the flesh at the base of her spine.

"Thawn, my seabird," he whispered hoarsely into her warm mouth, "spread your wings for me."

She groaned and arched toward him, loving the feel of his hard body against her softness. He deftly peeled up her sweater and tossed it aside, then pulled her with

him down onto the cool, soft sand.

The ocean was a distant roar as they lay, protected, in their special hiding place. The sand seemed to melt away from Thawn's bare back, holding her in a bed of magic. The chilly air that filtered in through the vents was warm when it reached them. All of nature seemed to be doing its part to create the spell that held them.

Thawn lay back and watched Rafe caress her breasts, teasing the nipples until they formed hard, dark sentinels against the creamy skin. She reached to dig her fingers into his dark hair, to pull his mouth down to finish the job his fingers had begun.

"Rafe," she gasped. "Oh Rafe!"

He raised his head, and she was stunned by the depth of desire in his stormy eyes. She'd never seen anything like it before. It frightened her but aroused her as well, and she found her hands reaching for his shirt and pulling at the buttons to make way for her own exploration.

His dark chest hair intrigued her. She pushed her fingers through it, curling strands about her fingers. She thrust her body against his, wanting to feel the crisp, rough hair against her nipples.

His hands were like flames, drawing patterns of fire across her body. She turned beneath them, twisting to the pulse they created.

When she felt him fumbling for the zipper on her pants, she arched to help him rid her of her final covering. His strong fingers touched her, and she moaned her readiness.

"Love me, Rafe," she cried aloud. "Love me now."

With a new urgency, he rose and stripped off the rest of his clothes, then stood towering over her for a brief moment. She thrilled at the sight of him, his magnificent body ready for her. Then he came to her and took her

against him, gently but firmly so that she was pressed against all of his long, glorious length. She looked up and their eyes locked, sultry with passion. She began to writhe, calling his name, sharing his triumph as she wrapped her arms and legs around him and pulled him ever closer. At her insistent urging, he followed her command, and she gasped, shivering with response, as he took control and joined their bodies with a sure and powerful movement.

Their union was like a wave caught at the apex, a wild ride in an angry sea. It swept her along and threw her high against the clouds, but when she came down again, Rafe was there to catch her.

She lay with her head against his wide, bare chest. The rhythm of his breathing had finally slowed. She could almost think he was asleep, but he moved beneath her, and she realized he was savoring the interlude in the same way she was.

"So this is what one of your spells is like," he muttered huskily, forcing her face up to meet his gaze. "Tell me quick, what did I turn into?"

Happy laughter bubbled up in her chest. "Oh, no"— she shook her head—"I'll never tell."

He cast her a mock frown. "Come on," he coaxed. "All this magic and I don't even get to know what I did with it?"

She grinned, snuggling down against him and running her hand in tiny circles along his naked side. "What do you think you turned into?" she teased.

His grin was cocksure. "Oh, no, you don't. You're not going to trap me into being an egotistical braggart."

She laughed out loud. "Oh ho! So now I have some idea of what you think."

He caught her face with both hands. "And what do you think, Thawn?" he probed.

Suddenly the mood was serious. She stared back into his deep, misty eyes, then drew in a trembling breath. "I think I like you very much, Rafe Armstrong," she told him bravely. "Is that good enough for you?"

It wasn't. She could tell by his fierce frown. But what did he expect? He was famous for his lack of commitment. Did he actually want one from her?

Instead of answering, he lowered his head to nip at the peak of her breast. "Do you realize we haven't had dinner?" he growled against her satiny skin.

She pulled away from him and reached for her sweater. "That's not on the menu." She chuckled, and when his eyes met hers again, he was smiling.

"Hear that ocean?" He cocked his head toward the sound of the waves. "It's calling us back." His eyes lit with mischief. "Shall we go?"

They scrambled back into their clothes and tunneled out into the cold ocean wind. The setting sun had turned the sky a thousand flaming colors.

"Sunshine tomorrow," Rafe told her in a knowing tone, and gazing in awe at the peach and crimson horizon, Thawn believed him.

CHAPTER SIX

LEAVING THEIR SHOES on the dry, crumbling sand, they rolled up their pants legs and raced the tide, dashing down into the water as the white foam of a spent wave retreated to the dark and lonely sea, then turning back toward land with a shout when a new wave broke and cascaded toward them. Eventually Thawn was doused by a huge wave and lost the race. Rafe stopped to drag her back out of the surging water, and soon he was wet from head to foot as well.

They struggled to higher ground, bent over with laughter. This good-humored acceptance of whatever happened next seemed so much a part of him that Thawn was surprised she hadn't seen it before.

Of course it couldn't last. Maybe if she entered into the relationship accepting that, it wouldn't hurt so badly when the break came. Maybe if she kept reminding herself of all the other women who had hoped to make Rafe Armstrong theirs . . .

It didn't matter. She was fascinated with him, but that wasn't love. She just had to make sure the feeling didn't develop into anything serious. If she could.

All the while they cavorted together in the surf and across the sand, she held her doubts at bay. But she knew she would have to face them sometime.

"You're the sea witch, aren't you?" Rafe laughed at her as he pulled her, dripping wet, from the waves again. "What happens when a mortal takes the sea witch as his own?"

She shot a quick glance up at him. He was only teasing her. He didn't know how close she was to wishing it would happen.

She managed to smile. "Dire results," she warned with mock gloom. "The sun is struck from the sky." She pointed toward the dark horizon, behind which the sun had disappeared almost an hour before. "You see how powerful she can be."

He pulled her close and tasted her lips, then pushed his hands up under her soggy sweater, rubbing her chilled skin to warm her. "I know how powerful she can be," he groaned into the hollow of her neck. His hands cupped her breasts as though to guard them from the cold wool. "I'm only grateful," he said softly, "that she hasn't turned me into a toad, as she threatened."

"We're both going to turn into flotsam if we don't get out of these wet clothes," she warned. "I think we'd better head back to my place."

They walked along the beach side by side, admiring the silver sparkle on the black water as the moon rose. Thawn was shivering, but she wished this moment could last forever.

Her little cottage was dark, but she lit a lantern that cast a rosy glow about the room.

"I've got a spare pair of jeans in my car," Rafe told her. "I'll run out and get them while you start your shower."

She stepped into the steamy water and closed her eyes as the hot streams cleansed her skin and hair. She heard the sounds of Rafe moving around in her bedroom, then into the bathroom, but it never occurred to her that he might come into the shower until he joined her.

"Hi," he said, smiling into her open-mouthed stare.

He seemed so dark standing there with the brown hair covering his chest and legs and much of the rest of his body. Somehow he seemed more intimidating than he had in the cave.

"I'm...I'm almost finished," Thawn murmured shyly, but he reached out to help her wash.

"There's no hurry," he said softly.

She turned away from him, standing directly under the stinging water, and he began the slow, deliciously slippery chore of soaping her back.

"Too bad you're so dirty," he said huskily as his hands worked over her skin. "This is going to take a long, long time."

He turned her to him, and she didn't seem to have any strength to pull away. The cake of soap was foaming in his hands, and he smoothed the tiny bubbles over her stomach, his long fingers spanning the width from hipbone to hipbone, filling her navel with suds.

Then he began working up, rubbing the soap into the spaces between her ribs, then up and over her breasts, paying particular attention to the hard tips.

"Wouldn't want to leave any sand here," he murmured softly. "If there's anything I hate, it's sand between my teeth."

Suddenly she was laughing again. "Enough!" she cried,

turning from his caressing hands and back under the water. "You're tickling me."

He shook his head sadly. "What a shame," he said solemnly. "You washed off all the soap. I guess we'll just have to start all over again."

"Oh, no, you don't," she retorted, wrestling the cake of soap from his hands. "Now it's my turn."

His lazy grin told her he'd been hoping for just that. He stretched his long body before her, arching and purring like a huge jungle cat being stroked while she let her hands glide everywhere, braver with the soap than she ever would have been without it.

"You have the most gorgeous body," she told him happily as she moved over his hipbone and down across his muscular thigh.

"And the cleanest," he murmured, turning languorously beneath her touch. "I don't think you've missed a spot." He grinned. "But why not go over each one again, just in case."

Instead she moved in against him, reaching up with her mouth to catch hold of his kiss. Their bodies seemed to slide together, so smooth and slick, but the feeling made Thawn laugh because it was new and strange.

"It feels like someone else is here between us," she complained, stepping away to shower off the suds.

"Oh no," Rafe retorted, pulling her back against him. "Not ever."

His lips were warm on her neck, and she smiled a bit sadly before she continued rinsing off. What lies men told.

Stepping out of the shower, they dried each other with huge, fluffy towels and then dropped them to the floor as they reached for each other again.

"I can't get enough of you, Thawn," Rafe breathed into her wet hair. "You're habit-forming."

Thawn suddenly felt the chill of the night air on her naked skin. He was drawn to her. She could see it, she could feel it. But it was only a passing addiction.

She slipped out of his arms and walked quickly into her room, searching for clean clothes.

She was an absorbing attraction for him now, just like the films he worked on. They consumed him totally while they were in production. But once the editing was finished, did he give them more than a fond thought now and again?

He followed her into the bedroom and stood watching her with hooded eyes. Her pulse quickened. Was he going to stop her? Was he going to try to take her to the bed?

But no, his face was infinitely knowing. He didn't even mention his disappointment as he pulled on the jeans he had brought from the car.

"We never did have dinner," he reminded her quietly.

She paused while running a comb through her tangled wet hair. "Oh . . . no, I guess we didn't." She shot him an appraising glance. "I'm afraid I don't have much here in the house, and it's really a little late to go out. So . . ."

"So we'll have to go to my house," he finished firmly.

She looked up in surprise. "Your house? But you don't have a house."

His grin was satiric as he stood shirtless before her. "And won't ever get one if it's up to you," he reminded her. He went on before the protest that was trembling on her lips could find voice. "But I do have a trailer and a well-stocked refrigerator."

She wavered. If he was inviting her there, surely he

didn't have another woman with him. Why not go? Why not savor all she could enjoy from this relationship, as long as she held out no false hopes?

The road stretched out like a silver-blue ribbon in the moonlight. Thawn sat back in the Jaguar and enjoyed the sound of its roar as they cruised over the rolling hills.

"Are you staying for long this time?" she asked Rafe.

He cast her a questioning look. "This time?" he repeated. "I haven't been away."

She frowned. "Oh?"

"I've been taking care of the wrap-up on my last film from San Luis Obispo. I've been at the trailer every night for weeks."

A small, cold lump began to grow in the pit of her stomach. If he hadn't been back down to L.A., what had happened to the woman?

"Here we are."

As he pulled into the long, rocky driveway, she could see that there were lights on in the trailer.

"Rafe," she said slowly, "is she . . . is someone staying with you?"

His face gave away nothing. "Yes," he said shortly, stopping the car and switching off the engine.

She waited while he came around to open the door for her, then rose slowly beside him.

"Go on in," he urged her. "I'll just get my wet clothes out of the back."

She turned to watch him lean in to get his things, then started toward the few steps that led up to the entrance. Just before she reached it, the door swung open. A woman stood silhouetted in the trailer light, the same woman Thawn had seen there weeks earlier.

But she had only a moment to identify her. As soon

as the woman saw Thawn, she pulled the door closed again.

"Carly!" Rafe called from behind Thawn. "Carly, come back."

Thawn turned on him, furious. "How could you do this to me?" she snapped. "How could you bring me here to meet your lover?"

His eyes were cold and distant. "Don't be a fool, Thawn," he growled. "She's not my lover." He took her arm, forcing her to accompany him into the metal house. "Carly, come here," he ordered angrily as he pushed Thawn into the good-size living area and showed her to a chair. "Stay here while I go get her." He left Thawn to gaze after him in bewilderment.

The trailer was actually a medium-size mobile home, almost as large as a two-bedroom house. The walls were paneled in light oak and the furniture was Colonial American, with overstuffed chairs and couches and wooden sideboards. It had a warm, homey feeling that seemed at odds with Thawn's image of the way Rafe would live.

She sat gingerly in her chair, listening to the faint sound of voices coming from the next room and wondering why she was sitting here so compliantly instead of walking back to the highway in indignation.

Rafe had said the woman wasn't his lover. Then who in the world was she?

Rafe returned, looking more relaxed, almost relieved. Thawn heard movement in the other room.

"She'll be out in a minute," he said. "She's fixing us an omelet."

Thawn stared up at him stonily. "I don't think I'm very hungry."

He'd changed into a plaid shirt but hadn't buttoned it yet, and his dark chest looked inviting in the lamplight.

He began to fasten the buttons, then sank down into a chair next to her and leaned forward to speak to her softly.

"She wants me to explain everything to you before she comes out to meet you," he said earnestly.

"Wonderful," she snapped. "I quite agree with her."

His eyebrows drew together in a frown. "What's eating you?" he demanded.

"What do you think is eating me?" she hissed. "You come into my house, browbeat me, then take me out and seduce me on the beach, invade my bath, then take me home to meet some woman who lives with you. I've had a bit much today, Rafe Armstrong. I think I have a right to be angry."

"Seduce you!" His frown was fierce now. "What do you mean, seduce you?" He reached out to grab her wrist. "I'd say, if anything, it was the other way around."

"What?"

A beguilingly arrogant smile lit his eyes, and his fingers slid farther up her arm. "Wouldn't you call it seduction, Thawn? The way you led me down the beach, out where no one would bother us? The way you enticed me into your secret retreat? Like a spider spinning a web, Thawn, my darling."

He stroked the line of her chin, the curve of her neck, and she sighed as she felt a quiver go through her. She couldn't resist a tremulous smile. "A spider," she scoffed. "Thanks a lot."

His fingers tightened at the back of her neck, pulling her toward him. His lips touched hers so softly that she opened her eyes to make sure he was really there.

"Are you ready to listen now?" he whispered.

She nodded. What could he say that could destroy the warmth between them?

"Okay." He settled back and she did too, wondering

if he shared her regret at the quickness of his touch. How she wanted to hold him again!

"Carly is my little sister."

Thawn looked up in surprise. "Your sister!"

He cocked an eyebrow. "Can't I have a sister, just like anybody else?"

A slow, hot flush spread across her face. How could she have been such a fool! "Of course you can. I'm sorry I—"

He stopped her with a quick shake of his dark head. "That's not the whole story. Carly is living with me because she needs some time to recuperate. She was in a bad car accident a few months ago. Her fiancé was killed, and her face was badly burned."

Thawn felt a sudden rush of sympathy. "Oh, how terrible!" So that was why she was shy of strangers. And Thawn had been assigning her to the role of mistress. She could hardly believe she'd misread the situation so completely.

Rafe nodded absently. "It's been very rough. She . . . she's been going through a series of operations to correct the scarring on her face, but there doesn't seem to be anything to help her with the scars on her spirit."

Thawn was struck by the dejection she saw in his face. "She can't pull out of her depression?" she asked, wondering if Carly felt the same way she had after she'd left Mark. Her own experience wasn't nearly as tragic, but perhaps it could help her understand what Carly was going through.

He hesitated. "I don't know if it's depression exactly," he said slowly. "She seems to have no interest in starting to live again. She won't go out. She won't let me have people here."

Thawn glanced toward what she assumed was the

kitchen. "Is she upset that you brought me?"

He wasted no time on tact. "Yes. But she's promised to consider joining us while we eat."

As he spoke, his sister entered the room. She looked about twenty-one—a young twenty-one, shy and reserved. She was tall and carried herself with a lanky grace that made every movement she made seem fluid. She wore her silky dark brown hair partly over her face, but even so, Thawn could see the ugly red scars that covered most of one side. Despite the deformity, she was still quite attractive. Thawn could see she must have been exceptionally beautiful before the accident.

She was carrying two plates in one hand and a steaming omelet on a platter in another. "Here, let me help you," Thawn cried, jumping up.

The young woman's eyes flashed in defiance, then she looked quickly away. "I'm only scarred, not crippled," she snapped, stopping Thawn in her tracks.

Thawn glanced at Rafe, who shook his head imperceptibly. What was he trying to warn her of? But she couldn't pay attention to his fears. Carly was in emotional pain. Hanging back and waiting for it to go away wouldn't do her any good.

Instead of retreating into sympathetic silence, Thawn moved forward again and forced the stack of plates from Carly's hand.

"I can see the accident didn't damage your tongue," she said with soft good humor, "or your sense of outrage."

Rafe made an explosive protest, and Carly stood as though frozen by Thawn's words. Thawn paid no attention to either of them. For some reason her heart had gone out to this unhappy young woman, and she felt instinctively that she might be able to reach her. She'd

grown up with a cousin who had cerebral palsy, and she'd learned early that the handicapped appreciated being treated with blunt honesty rather than with tender pity.

It was obvious to Thawn that Carly wasn't ready to welcome her efforts. She knew she was taking a gamble, but she felt compelled to continue. She began setting the plates on the table, placing each with the pattern just right. Then she turned and took the platter with the omelet from Carly's unresisting grasp. "This looks delicious"— she smiled at Carly's stony face—"but you only brought out two plates. Won't you join us?"

Carly's dark eyes flickered across Thawn's face, then lowered again. "Wouldn't I take away your appetite?" she sneered. "Looking at me is enough to make anyone sick."

Thawn withheld her angry retort, knowing that Carly had been trying to provoke it. Instead she reached out, swept back the young woman's hair, and studied the red scars that spread across her cheek and down around her neck "They are awful," she agreed.

"Damn it, Thawn," Rafe growled behind her, but she pretended not to hear.

"You won't have them forever," she went on. "Rafe tells me you're in the midst of skin-grafting procedures that will restore your pretty skin."

Carly avoided Thawn's eyes with sullen silence. Thawn could see that she wasn't going to talk about her problem with a stranger.

"Are you in much pain?" she asked softly.

Carly's eyes returned to Thawn, widened with surprise. For a long moment she stared at her. "Not really," she said at last.

Thawn smiled. "Good." She gestured toward the table. "Please have some of this with us."

Carly didn't smile. "Are you the environmental nut?" she asked unexpectedly.

Thawn stepped back in surprise but quickly recovered her sense of humor. "I guess I am."

"Do you know a lot about the animals on this beach?"

Thawn nodded. "That's part of my field."

Carly flashed a quick look at her brother. "All right," she said softly, "I'll get another plate."

Thawn turned apprehensively toward Rafe as Carly left the room. Wordlessly he sat down at the table, not commenting on Thawn's methods. She hoped he wasn't angry, but there was no time to ask.

The omelet turned out to be as delicious as it looked and smelled. Carly had sautéed shallots and mushrooms to fill the fold, then cooked the egg mixture to a golden hue.

Their conversation during the meal didn't sparkle, but it didn't degenerate into hostility either. The only time Carly really forgot her self-consciousness was when Thawn asked how she liked her little bit of coastline.

"It's so beautiful here," she said enthusiastically. "I love the fog in the morning. I love to watch it slowly fade as the sun comes through in the afternoon. And I love to watch the surf smashing against the rocks."

Carly's face became animated with eagerness. "I saw a sea otter the other day. He was lying on his back in the water. I swear he smiled at me. Then he dove down, came up with some kind of shellfish, and cracked it open with a rock he carried on his chest. He was floating there on his back in the water, eating away and smiling at me."

Rafe was beaming at his sister, his pleasure in her happiness evident. Thawn liked that. In fact, the more she got to know him, the more she liked him.

A wisp of anxiety made her throat turn dry. She was

allowed to be attracted to him, but she mustn't start to like him. She mustn't mix her fantasy of how she'd like things to be between them with the reality of how they actually were. If she did, she would end up in worse shape than Carly.

She volunteered to help Rafe's sister clear the table and wash the dishes, and Rafe left them alone in the kitchen. As they worked, Carly relaxed even further and asked Thawn questions and sought her advice.

"I found a sparrow with a hurt wing and I've got him in a box outside," she confided. "Do you know what I should give him to eat? He won't touch the seeds I've tried to feed him."

"Try bread," Thawn advised. "Soak it in a little broth first. But don't count too much on being able to save the bird. Not if the wing is badly damaged."

"I *am* going to save him," Carly said confidently. "Just you wait and see."

Thawn smiled. She liked Rafe's sister. All Carly needed was a little more contact with the outside world.

As they were putting away the last glasses, Thawn cast Carly a tentative look, then asked, "May I come and see you again?"

Carly looked up at her, clearly startled. "Why?" she asked defensively. "To get on Rafe's good side?"

Thawn flushed. "No. I'd just like to get to know you better."

Carly stared at her sullenly, then turned away. "I think I believe you," she said shortly, scrubbing hard at the counter with a dish rag. "I've got to admit you're different."

"Different?" Thawn put away the drainboard under the sink. "Different from what?"

"Different from all the other women Rafe has gone

out with." Their gazes met. "In fact, I almost think I like you, and I can't say that for any of the others."

Thawn wasn't sure she enjoyed being lumped with all Rafe's "other women," but she appreciated the compliment. When they rejoined him, she could see by the warmth of his smile that he'd forgiven her for the way she had begun the relationship with his sister. And when she said good night to Carly, she was rewarded with the young woman's first real smile. It gave the ride home with Rafe an extra element of pleasure.

CHAPTER SEVEN

THE SUN WOKE Thawn the next morning. Summer had finally come to the central coast. From now on the sky would be bluer than a jay wing, the sea a whitecapped azure. Once again the weather fit Thawn's mood. Rafe was her friend and lover, and nothing could be bad while that was true.

Rafe was her friend. She smiled to herself at the thought. He excited her as no man ever had, not even Mark. As long as she kept from wanting too much, maybe she could have the kind of exhilarating fling that other people had so easily. As long as she didn't try to turn it into something serious, she'd be safe from hurt.

For the next two weeks she saw Rafe regularly. Most of the time she could even forget that he came from the show business world she despised. Only rarely did his work enter their conversations.

He still spent some time every day in San Luis Obispo, the closest city, less than an hour away. His office there

had a direct line to the studio in Hollywood, and those who couldn't do their business by phone made the four-hour trip north by car or flew in to see Rafe in person.

"What are you working on at that office?" Thawn asked him one day, wondering if he would want to discuss it with her.

They were sitting on a boulder watching sea gulls fight over something floating in the water.

"I'm wrapping up my latest film," he explained. "It's in the final editing stages now. But mostly I'm doing preliminary work on new projects." He picked up a flat stone and skipped it across the waves. "Have you ever seen any of my pictures?"

"Aha—the loaded question." She grinned at him. "As a matter of fact, I saw the spy thriller you put out a few years ago."

"The Randago Twist? How did you like it?" His voice was casual, but she had a sudden intuition that her opinion mattered very much to him.

"I loved it," she said truthfully. "It told a good story and gave a sweeping view of Brazil at the same time."

His satisfied smile rewarded her. "How about *Edge of Fear?"*

"That I didn't see," she told him emphatically. "I don't like horror movies."

"But it was so much fun." He looked genuinely upset that she'd missed it. "I was really proud of the animated sequence where the dead rise up and—"

She held up a hand. "Spare me, please." She shuddered. "I'm afraid I can't appreciate the artistry in that sort of entertainment."

He tossed another stone into the sea. "Then I won't make any more of those," he said lightly. "Thrillers are my mainstay, what I do best, but I want to try every-

thing." He laughed softly. "Did you see *Remembrance?*"

She shook her head. "I don't think I did."

"Probably not. The critics tore it apart, and the studio limited distribution." He smiled. "It was my first try at a romance." Reaching over, he planted a quick kiss on her nose. "That was before I met you. I didn't know much about romance then."

She laughed. "Stick with me, mister. I'll teach you all I know."

He tossed another stone into the sea. "I'm counting on that," he said softly.

She gazed at him speculatively. "What is it like to make movies that the whole world goes to see?"

He raised an eyebrow. "It's a lot like making movies that only the neighborhood kids come to see, which is what I was doing before." He grinned at her grimace. "Actually I guess it's just like writing a book, painting a picture, or having a child. It's wonderful. Exciting. When I'm in the middle of a picture, I'm totally wrapped up in it, hardly aware that anything else exists. But when it's over"—he shrugged—"it's on to the next one. That's what's so great about this business. There's always another project on the horizon, something even more exciting than the last one."

She'd heard before that he worked that way. Everyone had said so. But they'd also said he was that way about women, too. When Rafe Armstrong fell in love, it was deeply and completely—but it never lasted more than a few months.

She was lucky to have him now, she told herself. Never mind tomorrow.

She'd put off telling him about her brief time in Hollywood for so long that now she didn't know how to introduce the subject. Her relationship with Mark, the

article, and her part in Mark's fall from grace—she wanted to share them with Rafe. But whenever she had a chance to explain, fear rose in her throat, cutting off speech. What would he think of her when he knew? Would he condemn her? She couldn't risk that. She put it off another day.

Time passed pleasantly. Rafe worked in the mornings. By late afternoon he arrived at Thawn's little cottage. Usually he took her back to his trailer. After he changed, they would lie nearby on a sunny boulder and talk or romp on the rocky shore. Sometimes they walked down to a sandier beach for a swim, explored the shops in the nearby resort town of Cambria, or took Carly for a drive along the Big Sur mountain road.

Often their discussions centered on devising a compromise that would allow Rafe to get his permit. "We really should get Tom in on this," Thawn told him more than once. "He's been with the company much longer than I have. Everyone on the board respects his opinions."

"That may be," Rafe retorted, "but how can you be sure Tom will be amenable to compromise? I have a feeling he won't go for it at all."

Thawn was afraid Rafe was right, but she felt she would try. And when she first approached Tom about it, he rebuffed her firmly.

"I'm not about to compromise my principles just so your sleazy Hollywood "friend" can put up some gaudy palace on the seashore, stomping all over an important ammonite site in the process."

"Will you just come out and take a look?" Thawn urged him. "Maybe you can help us find a way to make everyone happy."

"You mean make Rafe Armstrong happy," he scoffed.

"I won't do it. Let him take his case to the board on his own—if he thinks he has one."

"If you would just listen to his side..."

Tom stopped her with a hollow laugh. "It won't work, Thawn. He can't offer me quite the same incentive."

She bristled with anger. "Listen, Tom, I don't sell out any more easily than you do. And you can keep your damn help for your own self-righteous self."

She had reached the door before he called her back. She turned, still angry, but something in his expression made her stop to hear him out.

"You know how I feel about you, Thawn," he said awkwardly. "I don't want to see you hurt." He paused, as if searching for the right words. "I wouldn't have done this...well, I did do it..."

"If you have something to say, say it," she told him icily.

He looked down at his desk top and spoke quickly. "When I realized how serious things were getting with you and Armstrong, I decided to do some checking. I asked around about him—"

"You what?" she cried indignantly. "Whom did you ask?"

He flashed her a quick look. "I know a few people in Hollywood myself, you know," he said defensively. "So I made a few calls. And I found out—listen Thawn, the guy is no good for you. He's had more ladies who thought they were going to be Mrs. Armstrong than most people have mere acquaintances."

Thawn held herself very stiff, trying hard not to show how his words hurt her. "I have no intention of being Mrs. Armstrong," she told him evenly. "I know what I'm doing."

Tom rose and reached for her, concern shining in his

eyes. "The man is thirty-eight years old and has never had the slightest interest in settling down with one woman," he told her gruffly. "Why should he start now?"

She shook her head. "He won't. I know that." She wanted to say more, to rail at Tom, but she held back. She knew he was warning her out of concern and affection, and none of it was anything she hadn't already told herself, but his words beat at her ears almost physically, and she was sorry she had paved the way for such a painful conversation.

That afternoon she skipped the details when telling Rafe of her failure to get Tom's assistance. She and Rafe were swimming at the sandy beach on the south end of his property. On the lonely stretch, which was far from any public access except through Rafe's property, they had no fear of company. Tired of body surfing, they were lying at the edge of the tide line, Thawn on her back in the wet sand, Rafe leaning over her. His long, lean body was clad only in swim trunks, though he had carried tan chinos down to the beach over his shoulder. She still wore only her brief bikini.

Each small swell swept cool water up around them, making them laugh and sputter when it caught them by surprise.

"Of course he refused to help," Rafe murmured as he planted a kiss on the end of Thawn's salty nose. "He's jealous."

"Don't be silly," she protested. "There's never been anything serious between us."

"Maybe not, but he wishes there were."

She lifted her head as another foamy wave swept in, washing over her sun-drenched body, then turned back to look at Rafe. "You're being overly sensitive," she told

him. "Tom's never tried anything."

"Never?" He grinned down at her, and pulled aside the strap of her bikini top, exposing one creamy breast to the ocean breeze. "You mean he never tried to touch you like this?" He uncovered the other breast and lightly tapped each tight nipple. "Never tried to kiss you like this?" His warm tongue, curling around the cool tip of her breast, sent a flame through her thighs.

"Never, never, never." She sighed, arching at his touch.

"The more fool he," Rafe muttered, raising himself on top of her and nipping softly at one breast while his thumb and forefinger gently tugged at the other.

Thawn gasped and pulled his wet head down harder, digging her fingers into his hair. "I thought you didn't like sand in your teeth," she teased breathlessly.

"There's always a price to be paid for anything really fine," he answered, moving his hips against hers in rhythmic seduction. "And you're just about the finest thing I know of."

She sensed his quickening desire and tried to pull away. "Not here, you idiot," she whispered.

"Why not?" he demanded, his eyes alight with the glow of rising passion. His teeth tugged gently at her earlobe before starting a trail of sensation down her throat. "Why not do the most natural thing a man and woman can do, right out here in this beautiful setting."

But Thawn was adamant. "Someone might see us," she insisted, rolling out from under him just as a wave caught her full in the face.

"You see?" He chuckled and shook his head in mock despair. "Just retribution. It doesn't pay to shun mother nature."

"I'm not shunning her." Thawn laughed as she pulled

away the wet hair plastered against her cheeks. "I'm just showing a little respect."

"What are you afraid of?" he asked in disgust, sitting up in the now waist-deep water. "Helicopters?"

"Yes," she admitted, trying in vain to readjust her bikini top. "And sea gulls and sea otters and all the rest of them."

"Including World War II frogmen, I suppose."

"Them too." She fumbled with the ties of her suit. "Drat. Would you help me with this? You're the one who took it off."

"I'll help you," Rafe agreed readily, then reached out and unclasped the back closure. As the top fell away from Thawn, she cried out her protest.

"Rafe! Some help you are!"

"Don't put it on," he told her softly, pulling the flimsy beige-printed material out of her hands. "Walk back without it."

She saw the earnest entreaty in his eyes and bit back her protest. "All right," she said slowly. "If you really want me to."

He grinned. "I really want you to."

"As long as you let me cover up before we get in sight of the trailer. After all, you even have chinos to put on over your bathing suit."

He groaned. "Always more concessions. But I suppose that would be best. Come on."

They washed the sand off in the surf, then ran up the beach hand in hand.

"You look like one of those native girls in the geography magazines," he told her. "You look so sexy I don't think I can wait until we get back to the trailer."

"You're going to have to wait longer than that," she told him, laughing. "You're going to have to wait until

after dinner with Carly, when you take me home."

The stricken look in his eyes made her laugh harder.

"They say that denial makes a man strong," he grumbled. "At the rate you've got me going, I should be ready to enter the Olympics as a weight lifter by the end of the summer."

They stopped to put on Thawn's bikini top, then approached and entered the trailer, where Carly had dinner waiting for them. When they'd finished their separate showers, they all sat down to chiles rellenos and a crisp green salad.

"You cooked these chiles individually, didn't you, Carly?" Thawn asked admiringly.

Carly nodded. "You wrap a stick of cheese in a piece of chile, dip it in a mixture of egg and flour, and deep fry it until it puffs up. Then you drain the fat, cover the chile with a nice Mexican tomato sauce, and eat."

"And eat and eat," groaned Rafe as he took another helping. "At this rate I may qualify as a weight rather than a weight lifter."

Thawn made a face at his bad joke, but as she looked around the table, she marveled at how far they'd come in a few short weeks. She felt so close to Rafe that it scared her. And Carly had changed from a sullen, shy young woman to an open and friendly one. Now when Thawn visited, Carly chatted with animation on a variety of subjects. Little by little she'd begun to open up, telling Thawn about her past life, the childhood she'd spent with Rafe acting more as a surrogate parent than a brother. But she'd never told her about the night of the accident.

Now she joined in the discussion on how to appeal the permit denial. When Thawn told her about Tom's lack of cooperation, she looked thoughtful. "Would he really make that much difference?" she asked Thawn,

her dark eyes somber with concentration.

"We'll make do without him," Thawn told her, "but I'm sure he could really help us if he wanted to."

Carly picked up her water glass and swirled the ice cubes against the side, making a clinking sound. "He won't listen to either one of you because he's jealous," she said thoughtfully.

"Oh, I don't think that's quite right," Thawn began, but Rafe motioned her to be quiet, his eyes on his sister.

"What did you have in mind, Carly?" he asked softly.

She looked up at him, then back down at her plate. "I . . . if someone else were to try to explain our side to him . . . someone who isn't involved . . ." She stopped talking and took a long drink of water.

"Someone like you?" Rafe suggested slowly.

"No! I didn't mean me. Someone else." Carly put down the glass and closed her eyes. "No," she whispered. "I'm sorry, Rafe, but I just can't."

They stared at her for a moment; tears started to squeeze from between her thick lashes. "I'm sorry," she said again. She rose to her feet and ran from the room.

"Leave her alone," Rafe said in a low voice as Thawn jumped up to go after her. "She's got to get over this ridiculous shyness."

Thawn glared at him. "She's not ready yet. Don't make her feel guilty for not being able to face people." She rose and followed Carly to her bedroom.

She sat with Carly for a long time that night. They turned off the lamp and talked in the dark. Somehow that seemed to help Carly say things she otherwise couldn't have.

She talked about the accident, about how frightened she was of life, about how much it had hurt to lose her

fiancé. Gary Jarvis had been a young actor Carly had met through her brother.

"Rafe hated Gary," she said at one point.

Thawn glanced at her, startled. "Hated him?"

Carly nodded. "He was against our relationship. That night, when it happened, we'd had a terrible fight. Gary had come to get me at the house in Beverly Hills. Rafe was there. He accused Gary of going out with me just to get a part in his picture."

Thawn frowned. Had Rafe been right? Had Gary been using Carly? But what did it matter now?

"He told Gary to leave, but I ran out a side door and jumped into the car with him." She shook her head. "Rafe didn't know where I'd gone. Gary was driving like a madman..." She shrugged helplessly. "Rafe thinks I should be over it by now." She twisted her fingers together. "What do you think?"

Thawn took a deep breath. "I think you'll get over it in your own time," she told her slowly. "But maybe instead of hiding you should start thinking of establishing goals for yourself, things you want to accomplish in life."

Carly didn't respond, but Thawn knew she would mull over the suggestion. She knew Carly was strong inside. Once she found that strength, she'd slowly recover.

Rafe was waiting in the living room when she finally left Carly in the bedroom. Only one light was burning, and he sat low on the overstuffed couch, a drink in his hand.

"She's asleep," Thawn told him as she sank down beside him.

"It's time she pulled out of this," he said. "She's got to go ahead with the skin grafts soon, and she needs a better frame of mind for that."

Thawn nodded. "But she has to do it on her own."

He moved impatiently. "Then what are we supposed to do, just sit back and wait for her to come to that conclusion herself? I feel like I've waited too long already. Maybe if I took a firmer stand..."

Thawn bit her lip. "Wait awhile longer," she suggested tentatively. "You know, I might just have a plan myself," she said slowly. "I don't know how good it will be, but at least it's something."

She outlined her idea quickly. Though Rafe wasn't enthusiastic, Thawn considered the alternatives he offered out of the question. "You just wait," she told him hopefully. "My plan may just work—and accomplish two things at once."

Rafe drew her head down on his chest. "You're quite a lady, Thawn Carlton," he murmured into her hair. "I may just have to keep you."

She turned her smile up for a kiss and sighed with contentment as he cradled her face between his hands. His fingers caressed her hairline while his lips drew from her sweetness. She knew that she would cherish this warmth forever, even if only in memory.

"Quite a lady," he whispered again.

Thawn went to present Tom with her idea the next day. He was sitting in his office shuffling through piles of Geological Survey reports.

"Hi," she said breezily, having decided to ignore completely the way they'd last parted. "What's new?"

Tom looked up, his wide face candid with surprise. "Not much," he drawled warily. "What's new with you?"

"I have a favor to ask of you," she told him. "Oh, don't worry. It has nothing to do with Rafe Armstrong." She smiled brightly. "It's his sister."

It didn't take long to break through Tom's angry defense. Once she'd launched into the story of Carly's tragedy, he stopped muttering indignantly and began listening.

"If you'd just come out and meet her," she urged him. "She's opened up so much in the short time she's known me. But she needs some contact with someone else to help her see that she's not a freak, that people will still like her for herself, no matter what her face looks like."

Tom avoided Thawn's gaze. "I don't know," he said, frowning. "I don't know what good I could do..."

Talking fast, she finally forced a reluctant commitment from him for the following Saturday. Satisfied, she returned to her own office and closed the door. It was a long shot, but what else could they do?

The pattern of Thawn's days took on a pleasant rhythm. She made it a practice to run out to the trailer to have lunch with Carly before hurrying back to work. Sometimes a work site would be close enough to allow her to walk with Carly on the beach, where she pointed out tiny sea animals, and helped her learn the names of the tideland flora. On other days Thawn barely had time to bolt down a sandwich and share a few anecdotes before racing off again.

Evenings, Rafe arrived at her cottage. They often went back to the trailer to keep Carly company. Sometimes they ate what she had cooked; other nights they picked up a pizza or some hamburgers and took them along. They were really alone only late at night, when Rafe took Thawn home.

That was the time she loved best. As she lay on lemon yellow sheets, holding Rafe's dark head to her breast, listening to his uneven breathing and feeling his rapid

heartbeat, a lump would rise to fill her throat. What she felt for Rafe so eclipsed anything she had ever felt for Mark that she couldn't bear to think about it. If she let its significance sink all the way in, she would go into a panic. If leaving Mark had hurt so much, what would losing Rafe do to her?

She held him in her arms as tightly as she dared, and kept back the thoughts. She would save them for another time, when there was nothing left to do but remember.

"We need to celebrate," Rafe told her one night as he leaned over her, stroking her downy hair. "Let's go out Friday night, just the two of us."

Thawn pulled up to face him. "What are we celebrating?" she asked suspiciously.

"My victory at the board hearing," he answered with a flourish.

A tiny smile curved her mouth. "But you haven't won yet," she said softly. "The hearing isn't until next week."

He shrugged grandly. "Call me a cockeyed optimist," he teased.

"All right. Where do you want to go?"

He threw back his head and leaned against the headboard. "Somewhere wild and wonderful. Somewhere special."

A mischievous grin curled her wide mouth. "Have you ever been to the Madonna Inn in the hills below San Luis Obispo?" she asked, her eyebrows raised.

He shook his head. "Will I find it wild and wonderful?"

She nodded. "I'm sure of it. If you've never been there, that's where we should go. It's something special."

He dropped a light kiss on her parted lips. "Friday night," he told her firmly. "Just the two of us."

She hesitated. "Why not take Carly along? I hate to think of her all alone."

"No." He brushed silky tendrils back from her forehead. "She knows we need some time alone. Just the two of us."

Friday was a hectic day for Thawn. She'd been assigned to write an environmental impact report on a residential permit to build on a hill that was losing a war against landslides. The prospective builder had dogged her steps, trying to talk her out of every conclusion she'd come to.

"You could build your silly house," she finally cried out in exasperation. "I could ignore all the evidence and clear your plans. And I can almost guarantee the structure will begin sliding down the hill within six months."

The man shrugged. "That'll be someone else's problem," he argued. "I'll be out of the picture by then."

Thawn stared at him in awe. She'd met her share of unscrupulous people before, but never anyone quite so blatant about it.

"You know what, Mr. Beis?" she said at last. "I think you've done me a favor today."

He frowned, drawing his black eyebrows together in a scowl that showed he had no interest in favoring her at all.

"Yes, you have. You've given me the proof I need that I'm doing something of service to the community." She leaned toward him in mock belligerence. "It's people like me who protect the world from people like you. Now get out of here while I finish writing this report."

She would deliver her conclusions personally, just to ensure that no mistake was made. She wanted to prevent

Henry Beis from pulling any strings between her firm and the county offices. If she had her way, he would have to go through extracareful screening before he ever built a house in Vista County again.

Her run-in with Beis had made her late, and when she arrived at her little house, Rafe was already there, waiting for her.

Still, he was in good humor.

"I know," he told her as he wrapped her in his arms for a long, warm kiss. "I know what it's like to get so involved in your work that you forget the time."

Thawn pulled back and looked into his eyes. She was sure he did understand, she thought with a hint of sadness. When he was working on a picture, she was sure nothing else mattered—not eating, not sleeping, and certainly not the woman who loved him.

She showered quickly and dressed while he waited in her living room. When she joined him twenty minutes later, he was playing with the two hermit crabs in her terrarium, seeing which one could race the fastest to the other side of her coffee table.

"This guy in the green shell has definite potential," he told her. "The other one might as well sell himself to a cannery. The only way he'll win fame and fortune is in somebody's crab soufflé."

"What makes you think everyone is so eager to have fame and fortune?" she asked crisply.

"Of course people are. Fighting for it puts the spice into life." Rafe turned to her for the first time since she'd entered.

He didn't say a word, but his face told her what she wanted to know. Until then he'd seen her in jeans or skirts and blouses, maybe a caftan or two, but never

dressed for an evening on the town. He obviously liked what he saw.

She'd chosen a soft black knit dress shot with metallic golden threads that shimmered as she moved like a thousand dancing lights. The bodice was snug and cut low, coming to a V that exposed a generous portion of creamy breast, and the skirt flared to give room for sensual movement.

Thawn had piled her hair on top of her head in a cascade of sunny curls. A single diamond gleamed at the base of her throat, held by a gold chain around her neck.

"You're a golden girl," Rafe breathed as he came toward her. "You're a piece of sun torn from the sky." He stopped a foot away from her, his eyes shadowed. "You're so beautiful, I'm afraid to touch you," he whispered.

She basked in his admiration, but condemned the space separating them. "You must touch me," she whispered back, her eyes unwavering. "Untouched, I begin to curl at the edges; then I slowly wither away, until all that's left is a tiny pinch of dust."

His grin was crooked. "You win," he answered with mock indulgence. "You win again." He captured her chin and pulled her lips close to his. "What if I mess up your lipstick?" he asked, just fractions of an inch from her mouth.

"I put it on again," she answered, closing the distance between them.

Rafe's mouth was gentle and caressing, and Thawn felt her spirit open like a flower to his warmth. New life surged through her veins under the thrill of his affection. She'd never before felt so alive, so vital, so much a part of the world as she did with him by her side.

"The reservation's at eight," she reminded him as his hands slid down to find a resting place at the small of her back.

He smiled as he released her. "I'm tempted to say forget the reservation," he admitted.

She shook her head firmly. "You'll do no such thing. You're going to see the Madonna Inn. I'm looking forward to showing it to you."

CHAPTER EIGHT

THEY DROVE SOUTH along the coast, then inland through the quiet farmland of Los Osos Valley.

"Los Osos means 'the bears' in Spanish, doesn't it?" Rafe mused as the Jaguar purred along the country road.

"Hm mmm," Thawn agreed. "In Spanish days they shot grizzlies here by the hundreds. They dried the meat and sent it to the northern missions, where they were short on protein."

"The poor old California grizzly," Rafe replied. "They're extinct now, aren't they?"

"Yes. Everywhere except on the state flag."

They swept along the road, Thawn pointing out the six ancient volcanic peaks that were strung out from San Luis Obispo to the sea. Jutting from the rolling countryside like dark sentinels, they brooded over the landscape.

"The last one is Morro Rock, the huge landmark of Morro Bay," she explained.

"They are gloomy, aren't they?" Rafe commented. Then they were on the freeway speeding toward their destination.

"There it is," Thawn announced some time later, motioning for Rafe to turn off the main road.

The Madonna Inn was set against a hillside strewn with huge round boulders. The buildings that comprised the inn and restaurant stretched gingerbread turrets against that rough backdrop. Painted pink and white, the inn looked like a fairy castle set in the Western wilderness.

"Almost every room in the hotel has a different theme," Thawn informed Rafe as they made their way to the dining room. "My favorite is the Stone Age room. Native boulders are built right into the walls."

The restaurant was decorated in gilt and velvet. Plaster angels flew from the ceiling, an artificial tree in the middle of the room sprouted golden leaves, and native rock lined many of the walls.

"I've got to admit this is a one-of-a-kind place," Rafe said doubtfully. "And I think it may be better that way."

"Oh, don't be a spoilsport," Thawn admonished. "The inn is wonderful. Come upstairs and see the gift shop."

After the gift shop she took him down two floors to visit the stone wine cellar and confectionery.

"Chocolate as dear as diamonds." Rafe shook his head in awe. "And they get people to pay these prices?"

Thawn bit her lower lip. "I want you to do something for me," she said mischievously. "I want you to confirm a rumor I heard the first time I learned about this place."

He raised a dark supercilious eyebrow. "Name it, my darling."

"Would you find out if there really is a waterfall in the men's bathroom?"

His nonchalance evaporated. "A what?" he demanded.

She tried to hold back her smile. "A waterfall. I'm dying to know the truth."

He straightened his shoulders. "I'll accept this mission on one condition."

"Anything."

"That you promise we'll stop exploring and go up to eat when I come back."

"Done."

When he returned, he was silent as he took Thawn's arm and led her back up the wide stairway.

"Well?" she whispered eagerly. "What did you find?"

He cast her a baleful eye. "You don't really expect me to turn traitor to my gender, do you?" he asked in a superior tone. "There are some things a woman just shouldn't know."

"Rafe Armstrong!" she gasped. "Tell me this instant!"

His scowl made way for a wide grin. "All right," he conceded. "There is a waterfall all right. Damnedest thing I ever saw."

"I knew it." She beamed with delight. "Isn't this place fabulous?"

They ate at a linen-covered table. The glassware was heavy and ornate, the silverware elegant, the china painted with oriental charm.

"We're celebrating," Rafe told the waiter.

"An anniversary?" the young man asked.

Instead of denying it, Rafe winked. "Something like that."

Thawn hid a smile, knowing what was coming. When the waiter returned with a huge pink helium-filled balloon that said "Happy Anniversary" and tied it to Rafe's chair,

she laughed out loud at his astonished expression.

Just then the band took the dais and began to play light swing music. Rafe swept Thawn onto the dance floor in his arms. He led her through a series of complicated steps before settling down to a slow, seductive rhythm.

"We fit together so well," he murmured into her ear as they moved easily about the room. "When I'm not holding you, I feel as though part of me is missing."

Thawn tried to ignore the flutter his words brought to her pulse and the tight ache in her throat. Keep it light, she reminded herself. Don't let him know how much you care. Don't let yourself know.

They had barely sat down for a final cup of coffee when a voice interrupted their cozy interlude. "Well, well. Look who we have here."

Thawn felt a chill. She recognized the vindictive tone before she'd turned to see who was so surprised to find her.

"Matty," she said without enthusiasm, greeting the woman who had worked with Mark so closely in the old days. "How nice to see you."

Matty looked the same, her short brown hair cut in a boyish bob, her green eyes alight with malice. Her companion was a young man Thawn had never met before.

"This is Jeff," she told them both casually. "We were just driving by."

"Hello, Matty," Rafe said, glancing curiously at Thawn at the same time. "You two know each other?"

Thawn's mouth went dry. She'd known it was a mistake to try to keep the past out of their relationship. Of course it had had to enter at some point, but she wished now that she'd been the one to bring it up.

Matty saved her the trouble of explaining. "Of course

we know each other. Thawn and I go way back, don't we, sweetheart?"

"I wouldn't say that exactly," Thawn tried to protest, but Matty laughed harshly, drowning out her words.

"Sure we do. Why honey, Hollywood hasn't been the same since you left. And neither has Mark." Her eyes crackled with angry intensity. "That wasn't a very nice thing you did to him, you know. It took him a long time to recover."

Thawn threw a quick glance to Rafe and found him frowning in bewilderment, looking from one woman to the other as though he had dropped in on a conversation in a foreign language.

Matty cocked an eyebrow at him. "But now you're after bigger fish, I see," she said sardonically. "A little swordfish like Mark is nothing compared to spearing a big bad shark like Rafe." From her smile she appeared brightly unconcerned as she added maliciously, "That is, if you really think you've got the bait for it." Stepping around the table to stand beside Rafe, she patted him smartly on the shoulder. "Keep up your guard, sweetie. And don't tell this little lady anything you don't want to see in tomorrow's paper."

Thawn went cold, anticipating what Matty might say next. Would she mention the article, spell it all out so that Rafe heard every dirty detail?

Rafe stood and glared at the woman. "Listen, Matty," he said sternly, "I know how much you like pitting people against each other. But if you've got accusations to make, say them out in the open. I can't stand this sort of in-nuendo."

"Oh no, no." She backed away, laughing. "I believe in the old adage, 'If you've got nothing nice to say . . .'"
She smiled at Thawn, then turned and linked arms with

her companion. "Jeff and I are just on our way home from a nice little vacation in San Francisco. We'll be on our way now." She licked her lips. "Anything you'd like me to say to Mark for you, Thawn?" she asked innocently. "I'll be seeing him soon. I'm sure he'd love to hear from you."

Thawn felt as if her world had collapsed around her. "No, Matty," she answered wearily. "I have nothing to say to either one of you."

"Ta ta." Blowing her a sarcastic kiss, Matty left the room with Jeff following behind.

After rising to see them off, Rafe lowered his long frame slowly back into his seat. Thawn found herself unable to meet his gaze.

"Just what in hell is going on here?" His voice was low and even.

Thawn reached for her coffee cup and twisted her fingers around the handle. What could she say?

"I thought you looked familiar the first time we met," he went on softly. "But when I brought it up, you claimed we'd never known one another."

"We never had."

"But you were in Hollywood. We know some of the same people."

She closed her eyes. "Yes."

He reached out and curled his fingers around her chin, forcing her face up to meet his puzzled gaze. "Why did you try to hide that from me?"

What could she say? Would he understand how painful that time was to her, how much she wanted to- avoid reliving the memories?

"I think we need to have a long talk, Thawn," he said softly. "Let's get out of here and go someplace where we can discuss this."

* * *

The long, low sports car took them back out over Highway One toward the coast. Neither of them spoke as they sped through the night, the dry breeze blowing their hair. A little north of Cambria Rafe pulled the car to the side of the road and turned to Thawn.

"Do you want to walk on the beach?"

She looked out at the inky sea and along the blue-gray shore. "All right," she said dully. She opened the car door and began to walk. She felt numb, as though nothing more could happen. He was sure to turn away from her now.

Rafe followed her across the sand, past piles of driftwood, down to the water's edge.

"Who is this Mark she was talking about?" he finally asked.

"Mark Lund. I think you know him."

He let out a deep breath very slowly. "Yes," he said coldly. "I know him pretty well. He's a promising talent."

She nodded. "I'm sure he'll go far."

Slipping off their shoes, they began to stroll just out of reach of the cool water.

"Were you and he . . . close?"

"Yes, very close," she answered, raising her face to the silver moon. "We were even talking about getting married."

Rafe was silent for a moment or two. "What happened?"

Even now she didn't feel capable of filling in the details. "It just didn't work out. We went our separate ways."

"Then why is Matty so bitter?"

Because of the article, of course, because of what it

had done to Mark's career. Thawn glanced at Rafe. Would he understand how she'd been tricked into giving the interview? Deep in her heart she doubted it. She remembered his antagonism the first day she'd come to his land, when he'd thought she was a member of the press. He had a natural antipathy for people who tried to delve into his private life. He wouldn't understand how she could have been so stupid as to reveal Mark to the world. Guilt consumed her at the evasion, but she couldn't risk telling him.

She shook her head. "You'll have to ask her that yourself. Matty is a very strange woman. I wouldn't begin to try to analyze her motives."

"You're certainly right there," he said. Then his arm was curling around her shoulders. "Did we know each other before? I can't imagine that I could have talked to you once and not tried to take over your life within minutes of our meeting."

She smiled wanly. "I think you're exaggerating," she accused. "After all, you didn't want to take over my life after our first real meeting on your property."

He chuckled softly. "I may not have done anything, but I was certainly thinking about it." He pulled her around to face him. "Thawn, you're different from any other woman I've ever known. I saw that from the first. Don't you know how special you are to me?"

She was glad she meant something to him, but she wished she believed it would last. "Am I as special as those gorgeous women I used to see on your arm at parties?" she asked lightly.

He frowned, searching her eyes. "So we have seen each other at parties," he said softly. "I knew it."

"Oh, sure." She shrugged out of his embrace and began marching up the sand with Rafe following close

behind her. "We saw each other at parties. Though *saw* may not be the right term. How you could *see* anything through the throng of women that hung around you, I'll never know. I, on the other hand, had a clear view."

"Did you now?" He gripped her arm and slowed her pace. "If you could see me so clearly, why did you neglect to mention when we first met that you knew all about me?"

"Would it have made any difference?" she asked, trying to shake him away. "Would you have enjoyed talking about the good old days?"

He pulled her around to face him, and she found herself looking into his dark eyes, haunted by moonlight shadows. "Is that it?" he asked softly. His voice was almost drowned in the roar of the ocean surf. "Did something or someone in Hollywood hurt you so badly that you didn't want to be reminded?"

She reached up and cupped his cheek with her cool hand. Who was this man? Was he the sensitive, thoughtful lover she knew? Or was he the arrogant man she'd thought she'd recognized much earlier?

She loved him. She could no longer pretend otherwise. And she ached to let him know. But how would he react to such a declaration? Would it amuse him or scare him away?

The wind off the ocean whipped Thawn's hair across her face and flattened the skirt of her dress against her legs. She lifted her face to the breeze, closed her eyes, and waited.

Rafe stood still for a moment, then reached for her. "I hate to think of you being hurt," he whispered into the hollow behind her ear. "I want to make it up to you."

She turned into his caress, allowing him to taste her trembling lips, then force them gently apart for his pen-

etration. As his tongue entered her mouth, a flood of warmth rushed through her body, fighting off the cold sea air blowing about them.

She sighed, then gasped as his tongue became more intimate, more knowing, searching to ignite every hidden sensation. His arms wound around her like steel bands, holding her to him with a fierceness that almost frightened her, while his kiss branded his sense of possession on her in a way that would not soon fade.

"Oh, Rafe," she moaned, and suddenly for no reason that she could think of, tears were springing from her eyes.

"Hey." He pulled back, then leaned forward to catch each drop with his tongue as it ran down her cheeks. "What is it, darling?"

But she couldn't tell him. She didn't even know herself. She merely shook her head in mute surrender, and he gathered her up in his arms and carried her, curled against his chest, across the sand and back to the car.

"I'm going to take care of you, Thawn," he promised as he settled her into the plush seat. "I'm going to take you home, give you a warm bath, and sing you lullabies until you fall asleep."

She managed a tremulous smile. "If you promise to skip the singing, I'll do whatever you want," she said shakily.

He rewarded her return to good humor with a flash of white teeth in a wide grin. "It's a deal," he said as he lowered his long body into the driver's seat. "But don't think I'm going to forget your denigration of my talent."

He shifted gears and brought the long, low car back onto the highway. Thawn glanced at his serious face as he watched for oncoming traffic and felt an emotion

rising in her that was almost overwhelming. She loved him so. How had she been so careless as to let him take such complete possession of her heart? She'd walked into the relationship with her eyes open, knowing all the risks, yet that knowledge hadn't saved her.

She leaned her head back and sighed, closing her eyes. She could never have all of him forever, but knowing that would make her treasure their brief time together all the more.

CHAPTER NINE

THE NEXT DAY Tom showed up at the entrance to Rafe's property, just as he had promised. Thawn was waiting by the highway to waylay him and lead him down a path that couldn't be seen from the trailer.

"I don't know what good this is going to do," he grumbled as he walked beside her. "I feel like a fool."

"You'll get another little gold star to put by your name in heaven," Thawn told him, smiling. "Come on. I'll show you where to wait."

She took him to a rocky shore area pockmarked with tidal pools. "Stand right here, around this boulder, where Carly won't be able to see you until she's almost on top of you."

Tom frowned like a grouchy grizzly bear. "You'd better not take too long," he warned Thawn. "I'm not going to stand around here all day waiting."

"Just don't wander away!" she cautioned before

119

throwing him a quick smile and running back up toward the road.

Rafe had been informed of her plan, but he didn't like it much. "I don't want that guy hanging around you," he'd argued. But Thawn hadn't paid any attention.

"Your sister has to make some contact with the outside world," she'd stated firmly. "If she doesn't, she'll become more and more withdrawn from life."

He had agreed with that but wished she would use someone other than Tom. "Why don't we just take her into town to see a movie or something like that?" he'd suggested.

She'd shrugged. "That's a good idea, but we'll do it after I try this."

Now, when she arrived at the trailer, Rafe was almost as grouchy as Tom had been. He cast her dark looks from his seat by the window.

"Carly," Thawn said brightly, "I think I saw a sea otter down by the rocks when I came in. Want to go down with me and take a look?"

Carly turned, her face alight with pleasure. "Oh . . . I'd love to, but right now I'm in the middle of beating egg whites for this angel food cake. Maybe in about half an hour."

Thawn whirled and glared meaningfully at Rafe, who gaped at her with indignation. "You're kidding!" he mouthed. She nodded emphatically.

With infinite reluctance he rose slowly from his chair and strode into the little kitchen. "Here," he said roughly, "give me that beater. I'll do it. You go on with Thawn."

"You'll beat the eggs?" Carly stared at him, nonplussed. "I didn't think you knew a white from a yolk, unless it was looking at you from a plate, sunny-side up."

Rafe shot Thawn another scowl. "Just get on out of here," he growled. Carly dropped him a quick kiss as she whirled by.

Outside, the sun was shining on the water, turning it golden in the morning light. There wasn't a cloud in the blue sky, and the scent of summer flowers mixed with the salty tang of the sea.

"Where did you see the otter?" Carly asked as she bounded ahead. Dressed in white shorts and a yellow tank top, she looked as long limbed as a spring colt. Her growing affection for Thawn had made her less self-conscious, and she rarely bothered to try to hide her scars with her hair.

"Over this way." Thawn pointed down the beach. "Near those rocks." She hung back as Carly ran on, crossing her fingers and hoping against hope.

As Carly rounded the corner behind which Thawn knew Tom was waiting, Thawn stopped and held her breath. She half-expected to hear Carly scream. For a long moment there was no sound but the rushing of cool green water as it raced up the sand and the screaming of gulls as they fought the wind off the sea.

The silence had lasted too long. Had everything gone so perfectly Carly and Tom were chattering like long-lost friends? Thawn could hardly believe it. She hurried toward the rocks.

Just before she reached the corner, Tom appeared. "Tom!" she cried, craning her neck to see if Carly was following him. "What happened?" she hissed when she saw no sign of the girl.

"Nothing." He shrugged. "She came around the rock, gave me one startled look, and took off like a gazelle. She's out beyond the point by now, somewhere out on that breakdown."

Thawn shaded her eyes but saw nothing. "Why didn't you stop her?" she cried. "You were supposed to get her involved in looking for sea otters."

He snorted. "How could I get her involved in anything when she didn't even wait to make eye contact?" He began walking morosely back toward the highway. "I'm going home."

Thawn ran up behind him and caught his arm. "You're doing no such thing!" she insisted. "Go out there on the point and find her. For all you know she might be about to jump into the sea. Hurry and make sure she's okay."

"Aw, Thawn," he groaned, "give me a break."

She fixed him with a stern stare. "Did you see her? Did you see how shy she is? What are you afraid of?"

He rolled his eyes heavenward. "I'm not afraid," he insisted gruffly.

"Then go on out there," she coaxed. "Do it for me. For our friendship."

He looked down at her in disgust. "I'll give it one more try," he conceded, "but that will be the end of it."

She smiled her thanks as he turned and marched toward the pile of rocks that jutted into the sea. Turning, she saw Rafe standing on the rise, watching. She waved and began scrambling up the cliff face to reach him.

"Hi," she said, breathless as she drew near. "How're the egg whites?"

He gave her a half-smile. "The egg whites aren't doing any better than your friend Tom is." His eyes were full of questions she couldn't quite read.

"He'll be okay," she said with more optimism than she felt. "He's going out to find her on the point."

When Rafe made no comment, she looked back at him. "What's wrong with the egg whites?"

He shrugged. "I'm not sure. I think they may need

artificial respiration. They look pretty flat."

"Come on." She linked arms with him and they turned back toward the trailer. "I'll see if I can provide first aid."

Once they were back in the kitchen, Thawn went through the motions of teaching Rafe all about egg whites, babbling on and on while he sat silently watching the clock. She knew he wanted to go after his sister, but that at the same time he wanted to leave her alone. The war that was being waged inside him didn't improve his disposition.

"If you've got powdered sugar around here somewhere, I'll go ahead and start the icing," Thawn said as the trailer door flew open and slammed shut.

They both froze, staring at each other, straining to hear if Carly had brought Tom back with her. But she walked into the kitchen alone—and very angry.

"How dare you?" she cried harshly, hands on her hips, chin thrust out in petulant rage. "I thought we were friends, Thawn. I thought I could trust you."

Her dark eyes blazed as Thawn stepped toward her. "Don't come anywhere near me. I'll never forgive you for this." She cast a burning look of disdain at her brother. "Or you, either, for letting her do it." She glanced from one stricken face to the other. "How could you?" she demanded again. "Don't you think I'll find my own friends when I'm good and ready? Don't you think I ought to be allowed to take charge of my own life?" When Rafe began to speak, she backed away, shaking her head. "No, don't try to explain how she was only doing it for my own good. That won't wash. From now on, stay out of my business, Thawn Carlton."

She began to stride from the room, but Rafe caught hold of her arm and stopped her. "Carly, you're acting

like a spoiled brat. It's time you put aside all this self-pity and went back to growing up." Carly looked up at him, startled. "Since you despise any altruistic motives Thawn may have had, look at it this way—she did it for me."

Carly tried to pull away, but Rafe refused to release his hold on her arm. "We need Tom to testify before the board in our behalf. Thawn can't talk him into it, but you might be able to." His taut expression relaxed into a half-grin. "You've seen the guy. He's no more threatening than a huge teddy bear. He can't do anything to hurt you."

Carly's face mirrored the conflicting emotions that Thawn knew were churning inside her. Rafe pulled her into his arms and hugged her close. "You want to restore Grandfather's dream just as much as I do, don't you? Do it for him, Carly. Do it for the dream."

Carly buried her face against her brother's chest for a long moment. At last she asked in a muffled voice, "Is he still out there?"

Thawn stepped to the window and looked out. "Yes."

Carly pulled away from Rafe and faced Thawn. "Will you go with me?" Her voice trembled.

Thawn's smile took in both Rafe and his sister. "Of course."

Carly drew herself up like a soldier marching to her doom. "Let's go. I'll make friends with him. But only to get him to testify."

At the door she turned back. "Oh, let's take the camera. There's a whole colony of sea otters out on the end of the point."

Thawn exchanged a glance with Rafe, then left with Carly, her knees shaking with relief.

* * *

For a while the summer seemed to flow along cheer-
fully. Everything fell into place so nicely that Thawn
marveled at their luck. Tom and Carly shared a common
love for nature that bound them together from the first.
Soon the burly man was a common visitor at the Armstrong trailer. Though Rafe didn't warm to him—Thawn
suspected he was still wary about Tom harboring ulterior
motives—Carly seemed to sparkle as their friendship
grew.

One day Tom displayed a master stroke by showing
up with a dog and asking Carly to take care of it for him.
He'd found the overgrown Saint Bernard puppy at the
pound. Softhearted pushover that he was, he took the
dog home and advertised for its master. While waiting
for an answer, he was boarding the dog, whom they'd
named Brandy, with Carly.

"She needs a watchdog anyway," he claimed when
challenged by Rafe. "You won't always be around; you'll
be off making your movies somewhere."

Reluctantly Tom eventually agreed to talk over the
building plans and how they affected the ammonite site.
"I won't compromise my principles," he insisted over
and over again. But in the end he helped set up an agreement that satisfied everyone.

Rafe arranged for the architect, the builder, and the
landscape designer to come to the lot one afternoon. Tom
came too, and the five of them planned a new site, one
that would conform to environmental standards, take into
account the land's geologic features, and not disturb the
ammonites.

"This plan, along with a signed agreement from you
that you will maintain the ammonite site, ought to go a

long way toward convincing the board," Tom explained
to Rafe. "We'll have to wait and see what they have to
say about it."

On the day of the hearing, both Tom and Thawn joined
Rafe. Carly had planned to come, but she changed her
mind at the last minute. As the three of them sat in the
hearing room, waiting for their turn to plead their case,
Rafe reached over and took Thawn's hand, squeezing it
tightly. "Now we'll see if you're my lucky charm or
not," he whispered.

She grinned up at him. "If they decide in your favor,
you might have to thank Tom for it, not me." She poked
him in the ribs with a sharp elbow. "Now be quiet and
pay attention. You want to make a good impression from
the start."

Thawn presented the case. Tom backed her up, and
Rafe spoke with great sincerity. Finally the three of them
working together persuaded the board to move favorably
on Rafe's petition; and they sighed with relief.

"This is only another step in a long chain of require-
ments you must meet in order to build your house," Tom
reminded Rafe as they left the room. "But your application has been pending for a long time, and if we talk
to the commissioner, maybe we can expedite matters."

By the middle of August the workmen were laying
the foundation and Rafe was excitedly showing Thawn
each day's progress.

"You know, I think this is actually going to be better
than my first plan," he told her one evening as they sat
sipping wine on a blanket spread across the slab that
would be his living room. "The whole front of the house
will look out over the sea." He gestured toward the sky.

"The skylight over the living room will open it up even more."

She nodded. "Like living in a greenhouse," she teased.

He grinned down at her where she was sitting across from him. "I thought *you* were the nature freak," he said, reaching out to take her hand in his. "Don't you think you'd like living in a greenhouse?"

She avoided his eyes and tried to pull her hand away. "I like my little cottage just fine," she said evenly.

She wouldn't move in with him. She'd decided that long ago. He was a perfect lover right now, but it wouldn't last, especially not when she had to compete with brighter glitter.

Rafe raised his glass, letting the golden liquid take on a rosy glow from the sun setting over the water. When Thawn's glass joined his, a spark seemed to strike at their meeting.

"To our future," he said.

"To our future," she echoed, but she didn't think she would be sharing hers with him.

The sun began its slow plunge into the silvery sea, and Thawn shivered as the evening breeze sent chills across her skin. She was dressed in a silk blouse and pleated pants and wished she'd remembered to bring a sweater.

Rafe slid beside her and pulled her back into his warm arms. "You know," he said, playing idly with a strand of her hair, "I feel as though my life has changed completely in the last few months."

She turned toward him, searching his face intently, yearning to tell him how much he'd changed her life. But just then Carly's voice came to them across the ridge. "Rafe," she called, "you've got company."

Rafe held Thawn to him for a moment longer, gripping her tightly. "We'll talk later," he promised before letting her go.

They picked up the remains of their dinner and walked back in the gathering gloom of late evening, the lights of the trailer guiding them. Thawn wondered what would happen to the trailer when the house was built. A lot of things might have changed by then.

In the trailer they found a group of four men waiting to see Rafe. Thawn realized immediately that they were "in the business."

"Well, hello everybody," Rafe said, slightly nonplussed. "To what do we owe this unexpected visit?"

The four men stood up, grinning sheepishly. "Since you won't come back down to the studio," one of them said a bit defensively, "we decided to come up here and corner you." He was a short man, balding and nervous, but he seemed to be the spokesman for the group. "Listen, Rafe"—he frowned earnestly—"we've got to get going on this project if we're going to produce the kind of quality product you're known for. We can't hold off any longer."

"He's right," the tall black man standing next to him agreed, speaking with slow dignity. "You've been holed up here in the boondocks for much too long. It's time you got back in the action. We're here to bring that point home to you."

Rafe studied each of them. "You know I've been doing some work up here. I've been laying the groundwork for the next project. Harry, you and I have been on the phone almost every day."

The short man shook his head. "You know that's not enough. You never do anything halfway like this." His glance slid toward Thawn, then away again. "Whatever

you're into always takes your full attention. Now we all know you're busy with this house you're building, but the film can't wait forever. Some of the financial backing is starting to erode."

Rafe let out a sudden, warm laugh. "Okay, I'll listen to you." He drew Thawn to his side. "But first I want you all to meet Thawn Carlton." His smile as he looked down at her signaled to them all where she stood in his affections, and she flushed with pleasure even as she dreaded the purpose of their visit. "Thawn, these are a few of the men who make my films into successes. John Hunt here"—he pointed to the short man who had spoken first—"is my effects director. He makes sure we stick to the drawings on the story board as we shoot the scenes. Harry Barnes"—he indicated the tall man who had also spoken—"is the man who collaborates with me in writing the crazy scripts we come up with." He gestured toward the others. "Jules Tharp composes the scores, which would sell even if there were no production attached to them. And Manny Jones is my casting director." He spread out his arms. "Sit down, gentlemen. We'll talk."

As though his invitation were a signal, they all began talking at once. Thawn could plainly see the mutual bond of respect and affection that united them as they worked. She slipped away to the kitchen to prepare a pot of coffee and hunt up some sort of snack.

To her surprise, Carly was already there. "Did you let them in?" Thawn asked, pleased to think Carly had gained enough confidence to face strangers.

The young woman hesitated. "Sort of," she said. "When I called to you, I'd seen their car drive up. I left the door open and went to the bedroom before they made it to the trailer, though."

Thawn was tempted to urge her to take around the

tray of cheese and crackers she'd prepared, but then she thought better of it. Facing four men at once might be too much to expect of her. Instead she let Carly escape back to her room while she played hostess herself. But just before she stepped around the partition into the small living room, she heard one of the men saying something that stopped her in her tracks.

"The boys in the production group have a running bet, Rafe. We've seen you obsessed with a woman before, but we've never known you to stick with one longer than three months. We expect you back at work on a full schedule by the middle of September."

"I'm not waiting till September," another voice said with a chortle. "I've got my money on next Wednesday at seven A.M."

Thawn turned back to the kitchen, her heart thumping. They were right. There wasn't much time left. Biting her lip, she resolved to make the best of what time there was. Strengthening her determination, she put a smile on her face and entered the living room carrying the coffee pot and mugs.

The conversation had left Rafe's amorous relationships and moved to the business at hand.

"You can't convince me that the Western is dead," Rafe was saying heatedly. "What is the Western, after all? It's a morality play. And they never go out of style." He looked around at the faces before him. "I know Westerns don't draw the crowds like they used to, but that's because they haven't been done right. We're going to make a Western epic." He stood up and began pacing the floor. "Our story will be bigger than life. We'll take a simple human theme and magnify it." He ran a strong hand through his dark hair, making it stand on end.

"Okay," he continued sternly. "Begin with a young,

idealistic hero, someone the audience can believe in. Play him off against a cynical older guy who shows him the ropes. Have them come against obstacles that require heroic deeds. . . ."

Thawn listened intently, watching the men's faces. As Rafe spoke, their expressions were transformed. They nodded eagerly, and their voices rose in excitement. Something was happening that excluded her, yet she sensed the flow of creative energy and shared in the thrill of discovering new ideas. Suddenly without even thinking about it, she found herself voicing her own opinion.

"Characters based on real people confronting real human problems never go out of style," she heard herself saying.

Five male faces turned toward her, yet none showed any surprise. Each man nodded and contributed his own idea. All at once she was an accepted member of the group. She glowed with happiness as she listened to each comment, no longer hesitating to present her views.

It occurred to her that this was a very different sort of show-business gathering from the ones she was used to. This wasn't a group of glamorous people preening and posing, consciously attempting to project a glamorous image. These men were deeply involved in creating new ideas, developing original projects. They represented the heart and soul of the film business.

Thawn remembered what Rafe looked like at the fancy parties they'd both attended. His face had been stiff with boredom. His movements had been slow, his speech slightly slurred. Here he was different. His expression was alive, his words quick and meaningful. He was doing what he loved.

All the men he was working with looked the same way. They weren't driven by an ambition that made them

sell their souls. Theirs was an ambition to work harder, think more creatively, struggle more fiercely with an idea. Theirs was an honest labor.

Thawn's skin tingled as though she had made a discovery of major significance. This was good work. Rafe was an honest man. Why hadn't she realized that before?

She'd been so blinded by the hurt she'd suffered because of Mark's crassness that she hadn't allowed herself to see the truth. She could trust Rafe. He wouldn't lie to her. He wouldn't lie to himself.

She refocused her attention on the discussion going on around her. "You can't do everything yourself," John Hunt was saying. "You'll have to get someone else to take over some of the production work, some bright young guy with a fresh outlook, someone who will benefit from the exposure to your methods."

"How about Mark Lund?" Harry Barnes suggested. "He's one of the best around."

The name had shot through the room like an electric current. Suddenly two pairs of eyes were on Thawn. Rafe watched her closely. And Harry seemed to have suddenly remembered the connection between her and Mark.

The conversation continued, but she didn't hear another word. Harry knew. Would he tell Rafe about the article? Of course he would. Any one of them would use anything they could to discourage Rafe's interest in her.

She should have told him herself, but she was so ashamed of what she'd done. He would never understand. He would see her as a typical groupie who had hung around a star for the glitter that might rub off. He would consider her spilling of all the lurid details to the most sensational branch of the press only the icing on the cake.

She might as well face it. Soon he would know it all.

As unobtrusively as possible, she told Rafe good-bye and left the men still talking, knowing they would continue long into the night.

A great fear had settled in her stomach, as heavy as a stone.

CHAPTER TEN

A FEELING OF impending doom hung over Thawn the entire next day. Her job assignment was located at the north end of the county, in a town that wanted to rebuild a bridge over a stream in the downtown area. Determining whether the new plans would follow Vista County guidelines and abide by Coastal Commission regulations took her most of the day.

When she arrived home it was well into the evening, though not yet dark. Rafe's car was parked in front of her house, just as she had expected, but he was nowhere to be seen.

She waited at home for a few minutes, changing into a short yellow sundress before heading toward the beach to look for him.

He was sitting on a rock near the shore, watching a group of toddlers making a castle. At her approach he turned and looked up. His eyes revealed no emotion, but

he smiled just before she reached him.

Her heart was beating a sharp, painful rhythm against her ribs, and, afraid he would see how her hands were shaking, she hid them as she lowered herself to the sand beside him.

He knew about the article. She was sure of it. What did he think? Although she thought she'd inured herself to it, suddenly she couldn't bear the thought of losing him.

They both sat silently watching the children. She wanted to say something to bring the subject into the open, but the words wouldn't come. It was as though a wall had come between them, and nothing she could do would penetrate it.

"Another long day," he said at last.

She nodded.

"Come on." Abruptly he moved to his feet and reached down to help her up. "Let's take a walk."

She went along with him, letting his hand in the small of her back guide her. She hardly noticed that he had turned their steps in through the meadow rather than out along the sandy shore. Her thoughts were filled with dread.

"What's that?"

Thawn looked up with a start as he stopped her with his hand and gestured ahead. She looked to where he was pointing and smiled. "That's none other than the great blue heron. Isn't he beautiful?"

The bird was at least four feet tall, with a long, curved neck and a sharp beak. Wading in a marshy area near the trees, it was totally unconcerned by their approach.

"Are they tame?" Rafe asked incredulously.

"Oh, no. In fact, if he decides to acknowledge our presence, you'll hear the most blood curdling squawking

you can imagine." She glanced about them. "Let's detour around this way."

It was a relief to be able to talk about something so innocuous. "This is one of their major nesting areas," she babbled on nervously as they made their way through short grass and tiny yellow flowers. "There's a protected rookery down in Morro Beach. They fly in during early winter and make their nests in the tops of eucalyptus trees."

They were walking among the trees now, and Thawn pulled her arms around herself as the cooler air penetrated her clothes. She glanced at Rafe and found his face pensive. She was sure he wasn't listening to her ramblings.

Finally she couldn't stand the tension. "Rafe," she said bravely, placing her hand on his arm. The warmth of his flesh beneath the crisp cotton cloth made her fingers tingle, and she wished suddenly that she could feel that warmth against her whole body. If he held her, maybe it would all go away...

"Rafe, where are we going?"

They stood facing one another. He looked down into her eyes, studying her face with sharp intelligence.

"Tell me about Mark," he said softly. "Tell me what you two had together. Tell me why you did what you did. Make me understand."

Thawn felt as though all the blood had drained from her in one chilling wave. Swaying slightly, she clutched at his arm to save herself from falling. But he didn't take hold of her. He was waiting for her answer.

She licked her dry lips. "Harry told you, didn't he?"

He nodded.

"I...I should have told you myself."

He nodded again.

"I...the article was a mistake. I should never have

let that happen. I was stupid and. . . ."

His hands gripped her tightly, as though he were about to shake her. "How could it be a mistake?" he charged with barely restrained ferocity. "You gave the interview, didn't you? You told Jacqui Blatts all those things, didn't you?"

She gazed up at him with wide eyes. How could she possibly explain?

"Please, Thawn," he implored her. "Please tell me why you did it. I want so desperately to hear your side, to be able to understand, to forgive."

She took a deep breath. "Mark—Mark did something that hurt me terribly, and I knew that what we had had was over. When Jacqui came to my house to offer her sympathy . . . I just let it all out."

His eyes had hardened to silver steel. "Then it's true," he said flatly.

"True that I told Jacqui those things?" she said evenly. "Yes, it's true."

His eyes narrowed. "Harry says the rumor around L.A. is that you got a nice bundle of money for it."

She shook her head. "You know Jacqui doesn't pay for information," she said woodenly.

Rafe nodded slowly. "The rumor is that you were paid off by someone who was out to get Mark, someone who wanted to take him out of the competition. You complied happily because Mark had jilted you and you wanted to get back at him." His voice had sharpened. "Is that true, Thawn?"

She stared at him aghast. Was it true she'd wanted to get back at him? Probably. Was it true she'd taken money from someone who was competing with Mark for film jobs? How could he think such a thing of her?

"Is that what you believe?" she asked harshly.

He released his hold on her. "I don't know what to believe. You won't tell me your side of it. How can I trust you if you won't tell me everything?"

She looked down at the soggy ground beneath their feet, her hands clenched in fists at her sides. "What do you want? What can I tell you?"

He reached toward her, then dropped his hand. "Were you and Mark in love?"

"I told you that before. We were planning to get married."

"Why didn't you?"

"I already told you. He did some things . . . like sleeping with Glenda Sayers . . . and the other items Jacqui wrote about. I realized he lived by a different set of standards than I did. I couldn't accept his ethics."

He frowned. "What could he have done that was any worse than what *you* did?" he demanded icily.

"I didn't do anything on purpose," she protested. "I didn't take money. I just fell into a trap."

"I'd like to believe that," he said stonily.

Did that mean he didn't believe her? She shrugged. "It's all over now," she said, her voice shaky. "Why can't we just forget it?"

"Forget it?" He was angry now. "Forget it?" he repeated. His hard hand grasped her arm again. "If you can't explain your actions any better than that, I want to hear you swear that you won't do the same to me."

She stared at him, completely bewildered. How could she do the same to him? There was no scandal surrounding Rafe. What did he think she was up to?

He brought his face close to hers, glaring into her eyes. "Promise me you'll never give interviews about me or Carly," he said harshly. "Especially about Carly."

She shook her head. "Carly . . . ?"

"You know that's why I brought her up here. There are reporters all over who would kill for a story about her. 'Rafe Armstrong forbids his sister to see her boyfriend again. She elopes. Boyfriend is killed in crash as they drive from confrontation with Armstrong. Sister is scarred for life.' Juicy stuff for the tabloids." His eyes burned into hers. "Think you could get a good price for that, Thawn?"

Indignation sparked her anger. "What I did to Mark was inadvertent—it was pure stupidity. I would never do anything like that to you and you know it."

He let go of her and half turned away. "I've been hounded by leeches since I started in this business," he told her angrily. "Everytime you turn around, there's someone else trying to take a piece of you, trying to pick you apart for their own gain." His flashing eyes raked over her. "But I never suspected you were one of them." He turned abruptly and walked away.

Thawn spun around and headed in the opposite direction. She didn't know where she was going, but she couldn't go home yet. She needed to move, to take out some of her hurt and anger in physical exertion. She ran through the trees. When she reached the sandy beach, she ran to the water's edge and splashed along the tide line, heedless of the waves and the gulls that rose out of her way, complaining loudly. She ran on and on until she finally dropped, exhausted, onto the cold, wet sand.

A long time passed before she could gather the strength to return home. Her little house seemed cold and lonely now that she knew Rafe would never again fill it with his laughter.

But life would go on. It had after Mark; it would now, after Rafe. She set her shoulders with determination and began fixing herself an evening meal for which she had

little appetite. All the joy had gone from her, all the emotion, and she felt curiously flat.

.She got up the next morning and went to work as though nothing had happened. Everything went smoothly. No one seemed to notice her pain.

But she felt as if she were moving in a perpetual fog. People complained that she wasn't listening to them, that they called as she passed and received no answer. Her boss unbent from his usual frigid dignity and asked if she would like to take her vacation a little early, since she seemed to be at work only in body and not in mind anyway. She shrugged off their comments. She was a little absentminded, and she seemed to have lost her sense of humor, but she was all right.

She expected Rafe to call, if only to say a final good-bye. She thought he might have second thoughts once he'd had time to think it all over, once he realized she would never have accepted money in exchange for discussing Mark.

When the days dragged by and Rafe didn't call, Thawn tried to tell herself that it was for the best. They'd been headed for a split anyway. Why not now, before he had to join his fellow workers on the new film project.

She wondered resentfully if he thought she might give that secret to the press as well. Too bad he hadn't been a bit more careful to keep her away from the strategy session. But then he hadn't known about her supposed treachery at the time.

She felt very badly about Carly. Would Rafe's sister understand why she had suddenly stopped coming? One day, almost a week after the argument, she tried to learn something from Tom.

"How's Carly these days?" she asked one afternoon, stopping by his office on her way to the copy machine

with an armload of reports. Her attempt to sound casual apparently failed. He stared at her curiously.

"She's fine," he answered. "Why don't you go out and see for yourself?"

Thawn bit her lower lip. "Has she been asking where I am?" she asked softly.

Tom's unblinking stare was disconcerting. "Why? Should she have?"

"I haven't been around for quite a while," she said defensively.

He looked down at his work and shrugged. "Oh, really? I hadn't noticed."

So much for that. Thawn decided he was playing games. She would have to go there herself, but she'd be sure to choose a time when Rafe would be gone.

Excited by the idea, she couldn't get it out of her mind. The next day she skipped lunch and left work early to drive across the rolling hills toward the trailer.

Rafe's car wasn't there. Thawn wasn't sure if she was relieved or disappointed. She pulled her own car up to the parking spot and turned off the engine, then sat for a moment looking around her.

She had so many good memories of this place. A lump rose in her throat, and she hastily pushed open her door and made her way to the entrance of the trailer.

"Thawn!" Carly looked surprised but glad to see her. "I'm so happy you came. I didn't expect to see you again."

"Really? Why not?"

"Well..." Carly looked embarrassed. "You and Rafe...I thought it was over between you."

Thawn swallowed. "Did he tell you that?"

"No, but he hasn't mentioned you all week, and when he left for Hollywood the other day, I just assumed..."

She shrugged, then reached for Thawn to give her a quick hug. "We've become such good friends. I'm glad you're not going to let Rafe come between us."

Thawn searched Carly's candid gaze. The younger woman assumed it was over between her and Rafe. The pattern of his romances was as well known to Carly as to anyone else. She knew they never lasted, and as much as she liked Thawn, she'd had no doubts that Rafe would tire of her, too.

"He left you here all alone?" she asked, instead of pursuing the painful subject.

Carly smiled. "I've stayed here alone before. Now that I have Brandy, and Tom comes to check on me every day, there's no problem." She took Thawn by the hand. "But you've got to see how the house is coming along. You'll be so surprised."

It was amazing to see how quickly the workmen had turned a blank space into a gorgeous home. The walls were up, the roof had been started, the shell was almost complete. With a bit more work, a family could live in it. Thawn turned toward the endless sea to hide the sudden misting of her eyes.

"Isn't it wonderful?" Carly cried, dancing from room to room. Thawn was surprised to see her so uninhibited in front of other people until she realized that the workmen were all on the far side of the terrace, preparing to leave for the day.

"Wonderful," Thawn echoed, noting the sunken area in the living room where the solarium would be built. Rafe's plans would bring the best parts of the outdoors right into the house.

"But even better," Carly bubbled, grabbing Thawn's hand again, "is a surprise I've been saving for you. Come on, follow me." She led Thawn down the cliff to the

shore and then out toward the point. "Be quiet now," Carly admonished as they went. "I hope they're home."

They jumped from rock to rock until they were out of sight of the house and trailer, with only the surging sea before them.

"There they are!"

Hugging the rock ledge, they looked down into a calm cove cut into the sandstone cliffs by the waves, where a small clan of sea otters was swimming. Thawn smiled at the sight of two black-nosed babies, their curious, bewhiskered faces alive with fun.

"Be careful," Carly warned as softly as she could against the noise of the surf smashing into the rocks. "When they see people they tend to hide in the little caves."

Thawn nodded, watching the engaging creatures with pleasure. Their thick fur shone in the sunlight. She couldn't watch their antics without chuckling.

"I knew you'd love to see the babies," Carly said later as they made their way back over the rocks. "This colony has been here longer than the one Tom and I first found. I hope they stay for the rest of the summer."

"They'll probably remain as long as they can find a good supply of shellfish to eat," Thawn answered. "But you know how ravenous those little devils are. That's what gets them into so much trouble."

Carly nodded. "You mean with the people in the shell-fish industry?"

"Yes. As loveable as the animals are, some people wish they'd really become extinct. A colony can come into an abalone bed and decimate it in a day. The abalone fishermen can lose up to a whole year's harvest."

"I know," Carly told her. "Tom explained it all to me. But we're still on the side of the sea otter." She shot

Thawn a quick look. "Aren't you?"

Thawn shook her head. "I'm not on anyone's side." They had come to the turn at the top of the rise, and she stood looking out at the sea as she spoke. "It's a problem that calls for compromise, not taking sides and fighting."

"Sometimes compromise is impossible." A deeper voice spoke the words, and Thawn froze, her hand still shading her eyes as she gazed out to sea. "Sometimes it's better to fight it out and find a solution."

She turned slowly and met Rafe's accusing eyes. "Maybe you're right," she said faintly.

"I'll go on to the trailer," Carly chirped, running off.

Thawn looked up at Rafe, thinking how tall he appeared, how he seemed to tower over her, his dark hair swept by the wind, his eyes the color of pewter. He was dressed in dark slacks with a wide belt and a raw silk shirt that was open at the neck, and he was holding a gray sports coat slung over his shoulder.

She could detect no warmth in his face. It was hard as the stone on which they stood. Nervously she pushed her hair out of her eyes. "I thought you were in Los Angeles," she said.

He nodded slowly. "We're starting work on the Western. From now on I'll be spending most of my time in L.A."

She glanced at him, then out to sea. "Did you say you wanted to fight something out?" she asked, her voice low and husky.

When he didn't answer, she turned back to him. His lightning gaze seared her, yet she couldn't look away. The wind filled her cotton skirt and sent it billowing about her legs.

"Do *you* want to fight something out?" he asked at last.

She shook her head, her eyes still captured in his steely gaze.

"Then why did you come?"

She lifted her chin with brave defiance. "I didn't come to see you," she declared. "Just because you and I don't . . . I couldn't desert Carly. I couldn't let her think I didn't care."

His shoulders rose and fell in an elegantly disdainful shrug. "She likes you, of course, but she won't fall apart without you."

Thawn swallowed the lump in her throat. "She's still so shy. She needs a friend."

"She has Tom."

"Yes."

"She's asked me to let Tom take her down to Los Angeles for her skin graft next week."

Had Carly gone so far beyond needing Thawn, or even her brother, that she could run off to the city for a day with Tom? Suddenly Thawn knew that she'd been counting on Carly's dependence to serve as a link between herself and Rafe. Without that she had no excuse to come to the trailer. A wave of desolation swept over her.

It took all her strength to tear her gaze from Rafe. "I guess I'll go then," she said softly.

He didn't answer. She had to step close to him to get back on the path, and she kept her eyes turned away.

"Thawn."

He didn't touch her, but his voice stopped her just as effectively. She stood inches from him, waiting, her head raised, her eyes on the distant hills.

"What is it?" she whispered.

"Don't go." There was the suggestion of a catch in

his low voice, and she turned toward him, her eyes wide with amazement.

The hard mask had fallen from his face, and in its place was a longing such as she'd never seen before, though she'd felt it in her own heart.

"Thawn." His voice sounded oddly husky as he pulled her against his chest and buried his face in her wind-tossed hair. "Oh, Thawn, I've missed breathing in the scent of you."

He held her tightly, his fingers biting into her soft flesh. "I'm starved for the feel of you. I can't let you leave me."

A small sob tore from her throat as she turned her face to find his lips. His kiss was hot and fierce and determined. "Stay with me," he demanded.

She nodded mutely.

"Come on," he said roughly, curling an arm around her shoulders. "Let's go home."

The unfinished house cast a giant shadow in the late-afternoon sun. As they walked past it, the wind whistled softly through the rafters, creating a siren song. They walked on until they reached the trailer. A car was driving off. Thawn recognized Tom's dusty VW with Carly in the passenger's seat.

"She's really better, isn't she?" she said as they entered the trailer.

Rafe nodded. "Tom's been very good for her." He gestured toward the couch. "Would you like a drink?"

She didn't want a drink. All she wanted was him. But she nodded and sat down on the couch, letting him fix her a bourbon and water that she knew she wouldn't touch.

Instead of sitting beside her, he sat down on the chair

that faced the couch. He took a long drink of the amber-color liquid in his glass, then sat back, watching her through narrowed eyes.

She stared back, half-defiant, half-shy, not knowing what he was thinking, wishing she could throw herself into his arms and close her eyes.

"Okay," he said at last. "This time tell me all about it."

A spark of resentment kindled inside her. "All about how I plan to expose your private life to the world?" she asked tartly.

He shook his head. "I'm sorry I accused you of that," he said softly. "I know it isn't true." He frowned. "But I'm not sure I understand the rest. And I want to."

She turned her head, avoiding his penetrating gaze.

"Thawn," he said urgently, sitting forward in his chair, "I trust you. But there are questions only you can answer. I think you owe me that much."

Of course she did. She'd tried to explain before, but the words hadn't come out right. This time she would work harder at it.

As quickly and succinctly as she could, staring down at her hands twisted together in her lap, she told him what had happened—how she had loved and trusted Mark, how she had discovered the lengths to which he would go to further his career, how she had opened up her heart to the wrong person.

"I made a series of bad judgments," she said. "I seem to have a proclivity for those." She smiled ruefully, but Rafe didn't laugh.

"It's too bad it happened," he said shortly. "It put Mark's career in a tailspin for quite a while.

"It's funny," he went on, not waiting for her to answer. "When I first decided to build up here, I thought

it would be a perfect way to hide from the world. I thought I'd be immune from everything and everyone." His smile was almost bitter. "But nothing makes you immune from life, Thawn. Even if you turn your back on it, it comes up from behind and tackles you."

She smiled in agreement. "It seems that way sometimes."

His eyes were warm. "I guess it takes time to learn to defend yourself against it."

Thawn felt as though a tremendous burden had been lifted from her. He understood now, and he didn't condemn her.

He rose and put down his glass before coming toward her. "I've missed you so much," he told her softly. "We have a lot of lost time to make up for." He swept her into his arms and carried her to his bedroom.

She snuggled into his embrace, closing her eyes as a thrill of happiness washed over her. She placed herself willingly in his hands. She would have no more doubts— at least not for tonight.

He placed her carefully on the bed, then looked down at her, smiling gently. He seemed entranced by the picture she made with her golden hair spread out across the royal blue quilt, and she smiled back, welcoming him. With sure, deft movements he unfastened the buttons on her blouse and reached underneath to release her bra. She arched her back to him, reveling in the freedom of unconstraint and delighting in the feel of the cool air against her skin. Then Rafe's warm hand covered her and heat grew like a bonfire within her. He molded her breasts to his palms and caressed her nipples into hard, rosy peaks. When his mouth replaced his hands, she gasped as excitement flooded her.

In a moment he had removed the rest of her clothes.

Her heart pounding, she fumbled with the buttons of his shirt, eager to feel all his warmth against her. She ran trembling, restless hands across his chest, shoulders, and back, thrilling to his hard muscles and soft chest hair, overwhelmed with the shape, texture, and scent of him. Her breath came uneven as his hands and mouth trailed burning paths across her fevered flesh. Then their mouths met in a wild union as their bodies came together with sweet urgency.

"I love you, Thawn," Rafe rasped breathlessly against her lips. "You're mine."

He wasn't asking her, he was telling her. But this wasn't the moment to protest, to ask him to be realistic. She knew he only meant it for the moment, for as long as the pleasure lasted. And she was climbing toward ecstasy, too enthralled to think. They took wing together, and Thawn clutched him to her, crying out her fulfillment, holding him against her heart. She would never let him go.

CHAPTER ELEVEN

"I LOVE YOU," he'd said. Did she dare believe that?

She waited to hear it again over the next three days, but she was disappointed. Rafe flew down to Los Angeles each morning in a chartered plane, but he was back by eight o'clock. They spent each of the three evenings at Thawn's house. Neither of them spoke of the future or of what they would do when production started on Rafe's new film and he wouldn't have time to fly up and down the coast.

He seemed to want to spend every free moment with her. One night when she suggested that they bring Carly along, he told her no. "Carly's got Tom now," he said. "She needs a rest from the two of us. She's so much more sure of herself, she can manage on her own."

For Sunday they planned a picnic to be shared with Tom and Carly on the slope in front of the nearly finished house. Rafe went home to spend Saturday night with his

sister, and Thawn drove herself to the site the following morning. When she turned onto the dirt road that led to the trailer, she had to pull to the side to make room for a car coming from the opposite direction.

But instead of passing, the car stopped beside hers. In it was Harry Barnes, the tall writer who worked with Rafe, the man who'd recognized Thawn's name in connection with Mark's.

"Hello there, Thawn," he said, regarding her levelly. "I've been wanting to have a talk with you."

She could tell by his tone of voice and the glint in his eyes that while Rafe might have forgiven her for the article about Mark, Harry hadn't.

"How nice," she murmured. "What did you want to discuss?"

He frowned. "This is an awkward setting, so I'm going to be blunt. I wish you'd leave Rafe alone."

Despite her inner turmoil, Thawn smiled. "I see. Anything else?"

"I'll tell you why I say that. When Rafe is working on a project, he throws himself into it body and soul. He's a creative genius. The world recognizes that and expects it from him." Harry smiled crookedly. "Creative geniuses don't tie themselves down in little white cottages by the sea. Creative geniuses need space and freedom from mundane responsibilities in order to do what they do best." He shrugged. "In short, you're stifling Rafe. If you don't leave him alone, he'll never make the Western he's capable of making."

She licked her dry lips. "You think I should give him up for the good of the movie industry, is that it?"

Harry moved impatiently. "Come on, Thawn. You're a grown woman. You know the score. He'll never settle

for one woman for very long. There's no gold band in your future here. Let him go now, before you ruin him."

"Ruin him!" Her laugh was hollow. "I'd never realized he was quite so fragile."

Harry shook his head. "He needs his mind clear to work. I thought you might understand that." He continued to scrutinize her, but she refused to respond. "Well, never mind, Thawn. I don't think this little affair has much life left in it anyway. On Wednesday we're packing up to scout locations in Wyoming. Rafe won't be making many charter flights back from there. It would be nice, though, if you could see your way to making the breakup quick and sweet, so he can get his mind back on work." He gave her another stilted smile. "Think it over."

Thawn watched as he drove away, then continued on to the trailer. But after parking she sat in the car for almost half an hour before Carly came out the door and discovered her.

"Rafe was beginning to wonder where you were," Carly said, calling her in. "There's Tom now. We're going to run into Cambria and pick up some deli meat and freshly baked bread for the sandwiches."

Thawn smiled in response to her youthful exuberance, feeling suddenly very mature herself. Mature people made considered decisions; they didn't let their emotions rule their lives.

Rafe met her just inside the door. "Where've you been?" he asked, pulling her to him and burying his face in her hair. "I've missed you."

"It's been so long," she agreed lightly. "All of eight or nine hours since you last saw me."

"A lifetime," he growled, kissing her neck.

She pulled out of his arms and walked nervously into the living room. "I saw Carly. She and Tom were leaving to get food for the picnic."

She turned to look back and caught a puzzled look in Rafe's eyes. But he erased it with a smile and started toward her again. Before he reached her, she turned away and spoke quickly. "So you had a visitor this morning."

"Hmmmm?" He took her lightly by the shoulders from behind and kissed the top of her head. "Oh, yeah, Harry stopped by. He went to see his daughter at Pismo Beach and dropped in here to say hello."

Thawn tensed, waiting for Rafe to tell her more, but instead he had a suggestion. "Come with me and see how much they've done on the house this week," he said, catching at her hand.

She followed him reluctantly, dreading the approach of the move she knew she must make.

The house already looked magnificent, though it was far from complete. The area around it had a raw look, but Thawn knew the landscaper would soon correct that. She entered with Rafe, and they explored the lower floor together, he exclaiming and calling her attention to each improvement, she following and agreeing quietly.

"Look at the view from the master bedroom," he called from upstairs. "Come see how still the water is."

Thawn climbed the stairs as though her legs were made of lead.

"Isn't this spectacular?" He swept her up in a whirling embrace and waltzed her around the room. "Just wait until you wake up with a roaring fire going in the fireplace on a cold winter morning. We'll snuggle down under the covers and watch the rain fall." He dropped a quick kiss on her lips. "How are you going to like waking up to this view every morning?"

She pulled away and turned to look at the sea, afraid to speak, afraid to reveal herself with the tremor she knew would be in her voice.

"It's the same ocean I see from my bedroom at my home," she said finally when she could trust herself. She lifted her chin. "And I can see just fine from there."

He came up behind her and drew her back to mold her body to his long length. "We'll leave all the windows open when we make love," he said huskily. "We'll let the sun stream in all around us. We'll listen to the crash of the waves and breathe in the salty air."

It sounded heavenly. But she wouldn't be there to share it with him.

"When do you expect the house to be finished?" she asked.

"I'm hoping to have everything ready by the end of September. Of course, I'm going to be away a lot for about six months. But you and Carly can supervise getting the place set up, ordering the furniture...."

He went on, but she didn't hear the words. He'd said it so casually. He was going to be gone a lot for about six months. He hadn't asked her to come along. He hadn't even told her he was leaving Wednesday. For once she would beat him to the punch.

"Rafe," she said suddenly, stepping out of his embrace and clutching her arms tightly around herself, "my vacation is coming up in exactly six days." She turned around and met his gaze directly. "I'll be leaving for Iowa on Friday night."

His jawline hardened. "When are you planning to come back?" he asked with deceptive gentleness.

She found she couldn't hold his gaze. Nervously she let her glance wander about the unfinished room. "I . . . I haven't made up my mind yet."

"You *are* coming back?"

She sighed. "Rafe, by that time you'll be totally engrossed in your new project. You won't need me anymore."

The silence between them crackled with tension. "What the hell are you talking about?" he asked harshly at last.

"About you." She thrust her chin out defiantly and stared back at him. "About your women and your films and all the things that you're involved in. I've known from the first that this was a temporary affair. It's about run its course, don't you think?"

"No, I don't."

She managed an artificial smile. "Well, I do."

He shook his head slowly. "You're joking, aren't you?"

"No, I'm quite serious. All good things must come to an end. This seems like a nice time to end this one." She flashed him a quick look, then headed for the stairs. "Give my regrets to your sister and Tom. I don't think I'll stay for the picnic."

His hand shot out to stop her; and she knew at once it was useless to try to remove his grip on her arm. Instead she turned her face toward his in earnest appeal. "Rafe, we've had a wonderful summer together. Why can't you leave it at that?"

He gripped her shoulders with both hands. "Because I can't leave it at that any more that I can give up eating or go without sleep." He shook his head sadly. "Can't you see how much I need you? You're all I think about."

"Rafe, please...."

"What can I do to prove that to you? What do you want? Marriage? Okay, marry me."

The words gave her a certain thrill, but she knew they meant little. Even if he did marry her to keep her around

a bit longer, how soon would it be before he hated her for what she'd forced him to do?

She shook her head miserably. "Don't say that, Rafe. Don't try to buy me that way. You want me now, just like you want your Western epic." She let out a long sigh. "But when your movie is finished, you'll go on to something else." She met his angry gaze. "Can't you see that?"

When he released her suddenly and turned away without another word, she thought she'd finally gotten through to him. As she descended the stairs slowly, then walked out to her car, she had the miserable knowledge that he finally realized why she'd broken with him this way, and that soul searching could only bring him to the same conclusion.

She drove home along the seashore road, and as she saw the hillsides burned brown by the late summer sun, she thought of the autumn ahead. Everything ended eventually.

He didn't come to her that night. Her bed had never felt so cold. The next morning was Saturday, but Thawn rose early after a restless night. She was watering the potted plants that filled her kitchen window when the doorbell rang.

"Come take a ride with me," Rafe said as she opened the door.

"Rafe, don't try to prolong this."

"Please."

His eyes were bloodshot, with dark circles under them. She knew his night had been no better than hers. Her first inclination to refuse evaporated as her heart went out to him. She would do anything to erase the hurt from his expression.

"All right," she agreed. "Just let me get my sweater."

The morning was gray with the remains of an early fog bank that was just beginning to lift from the shore. Its filmy tendrils seemed to slither between the houses as the car took them out onto the highway. Thawn wished the sun would come out.

"Where are we going?" she asked.

"North."

She frowned, unsure of Rafe's intention. "How far north?"

He turned to look at her across the car seat. The weariness had faded from his expression, and in its place was a wicked smile. "A hundred miles or so," he said happily.

"Rafe!" She sat bolt upright and looked around wildly. "Where are you taking me?"

"I'll tell you, Thawn," he drawled lazily, the picture of triumphant self-assurance. "I thought over everything you said last night—about how we should stop seeing each other because I'm too unstable to maintain what I feel for you for any significant length of time."

She gasped. "That's not what I said at all!"

"Isn't it? That's what I heard."

"No. I...I wasn't blaming you. You can't help it—"

He gave a short, harsh laugh. "Lord, now on top of everything else I'm too feeble to control my own actions."

"Oh, Rafe," she wailed in despair, "try to understand. I wasn't condemning you, only facing reality."

He nodded. "Reality means I'm a Casanova and you're a trembling victim?" He glanced at her, his eyes burning. "That's your reality? I think you're looking at the world

through some sort of screwed-up filter, lady. And I'm going to do what I can to clear your vision."

She shook her head. "By driving up the coast? What good will that do?"

He shrugged his wide shoulders. "Maybe a lot. Maybe nothing at all." He grinned again, his teeth flashing white against his tan skin. "But if you won't give me a marriage, at least I'll get a honeymoon."

She looked at him sharply. "Are we staying all night?"

He nodded.

"But I don't have any clothes with me."

His eyes twinkled. "That's how I like you best. Who needs clothes on a honeymoon, anyway?"

Thawn sat back against the seat and watched the rocky shore turn more and more rugged as they climbed into the coastal mountains. The fog retreated, but low clouds hung on well into the day. It was almost noon when the sun finally came out.

Now they were approaching the large pines of the Big Sur area. Thawn loved it here, but for once the scenery gave her little pleasure. Rafe would have done better to accept her breakup of their relationship. Taking her on this trip would only prolong their misery.

Glancing at him, she caught an air of pleased anticipation about him that didn't fit the simple plans he'd outlined. Did he have something else up his sleeve?

"Are you planning to drive on up to Monterey?" she asked, digging for details of his scheme.

He shook his head. "Right now all I'm planning is a nice lunch with the woman I love."

He stopped at a small grocery store along the side of the road and returned to the car in no time with a large brown paper bag bulging with food.

"A jug of wine," he quoted softly as he stowed the

package in the back seat, "a loaf of bread..."

Thawn glared at him with mock indignation. "Don't put me into your little poem," she protested.

"It's too late," he announced as he swung his long body back behind the wheel. "You're in my poem—you're in my life."

He gunned the motor and took off down the road again, hunting for a likely picnic area. "The man at the store told me to look for a turnoff beside two liquidambar trees. Aha!" He pulled the car off the road.

The spot was perfect, on level ground screened from the highway by pampas grass but open to a gorgeous view of the sea crashing against the cliffs below. Rafe retrieved the bag of groceries and spread the items out on a blanket.

"The first meal of our honeymoon," he murmured, gazing at Thawn lovingly as he pulled off a handful of green grapes and handed them to her.

She moved uncomfortably, wishing she could figure out just what he was up to. "The first meal of my kidnapping, you mean," she grumbled.

He poured the wine into paper cups. "It was either this or straight from the bottle," he informed her. He handed her a cup, watched while she took a sip, then leaned forward to take a taste from her lips.

"Eat," she told him breathlessly, stirred as always by the passion that rose so quickly between them.

He withdrew reluctantly, and turned his attention to the food, eating with the relish of a starving man. They both ate heartily, then lay back in each other's arms to rest and enjoy the scenery. The potted cheese had been delicious spread on sourdough bread. Apparently even the ants thought so. A long line of them was marching across the blanket.

"Time to go," Thawn announced abruptly, standing up and shaking out the blanket. "There are some many-legged creatures in this would I can do without."

They stowed their litter in the trunk and drove on into the heart of the big trees. When Rafe turned onto a road Thawn didn't recognize, she glanced at him sharply but didn't say a word. Obviously he had a specific destination in mind.

Suddenly a road block appeared before them. Thawn sat up in her seat and looked questioningly at Rafe.

"Oh, it's you Mr. Armstrong," the guard said deferentially. "Go right on in."

Thawn's eyes widened. "What is this, Rafe?" she demanded as they sped through the barricade and rounded a corner.

"What does it look like, Thawn?" he answered, braking and switching off the engine.

She knew where they were before she saw the sound trucks, the dressing-room trailers for the actors, and the mobile film labs. This was the set for a movie being filmed on location. But why had Rafe brought her here? What was he trying to do?

"Come on." He opened the door on her side and pulled her out of the car. "Let's take a look."

They took only a few steps before Rafe was surrounded by people exclaiming over his arrival, clamoring for his advice. Thawn found herself being carried farther and farther from him until finally she dropped into a convenient folding chair and watched him while he and the entourage moved on down the road, toward where cameras and lights had been set up.

It was all so familiar—the frantic vying for attention, the pushing and shoving—and the achingly empty feeling of being hopelessly out of place. This was Rafe's

world, Mark's world, but never hers.

But Rafe had stopped. A head taller than most of the people around him, he had no trouble spotting her. She saw him frown, say a few sharp words to the crowd, and step away from them to return to her.

"I was keeping my eye on you," he said apologetically as he stood before her. "Don't think I forgot you. I could see you clearly from behind all those people."

"That was more than I could do," she admitted, walking into his open arms and taking his bear hug with a glow of pleasure.

"Come with me." This time he took a firm hold on her and refused to let anyone separate them again. Caught up in the excitement, Thawn found she almost enjoyed all the attention Rafe received.

He introduced her to the director, and she was surprised to learn that the film was a love story Rafe was co-producing. "You didn't tell me you were working on something besides the Western right now," she accused.

He shook his head. "I'm not really. I wrote the original story, though not the screenplay, and I did most of the preliminary planning and assembled the financial backing. Jeff Corwin is handling the line production." He held her gaze. "Jeff and a young assistant we hired— Mark Lund."

Thawn froze. "How nice," she managed to say before Rafe led her down the road away from the crowd, where they could talk alone.

"Why?" she cried. "Why did you do this to me? What can you possibly hope to accomplish by humiliating me in front of—"

Rafe took hold of her shoulders to quiet her. "Will you calm down and listen for a minute?" he ordered.

"What happened between you and Mark created a poison that's been eating away at you ever since. It's time you had it out and cleared away the debris."

She looked around rebelliously. "I don't want to talk it out with Mark."

"I know you don't." Rafe pulled her close. "But I want us to have a chance, Thawn. And we never will until you put your feelings for Mark to rest."

He glanced behind her, and she heard the sound of someone approaching. "Here he comes," he told her softly. "Do it for me, Thawn. For us."

He released her and left without another word. She stood where she was, waiting for Mark to step in front of her.

Outwardly he looked much the same. His blond hair still curled around his head like a wild halo. His blue eyes still gleamed with vitality. But there was an air about him of defensive reserve that he'd never had before. Or was it just that he hated her?

"Mark," she said stiffly.

"Hello, Thawn." He stood a few feet away from her and waited.

She swallowed and tried again. "I . . . I guess you're probably still angry with me."

"I imagine you don't have many good thoughts about me, either," he conceded.

She nodded. "Some things still hurt," she admitted softly.

They stared at one another, and the silence grew between them like a crystal wall.

Finally Mark broke it. "Rafe told me to talk to you. I didn't want to do it. I don't really see that we have anything left to discuss." He moved restlessly. "But Rafe's

been good to me. He hired me when no one else would. He believes in my work. And I'll do just about anything to make that up to him."

Thawn let out a hollow laugh. "Including being nice to the person you hate most in the world?"

He shook his head slowly. "I don't hate you, Thawn. I'm sure you wanted to get back at me when you gave that interview to Jacqui. I just hope revenge was sweet enough to—"

"No!" Thawn broke into his bitter speech. "I wasn't looking for revenge. I needed someone to talk to. Jacqui was handy. I never dreamed she would print everything I said."

He shrugged. "It doesn't matter. What's done is done."

She glared at him defiantly. "It was the truth, after all. You did do the things the article accused you of. What right have you to be so self-righteous toward me?"

His eyes narrowed with anger, and his hands balled into fists at his sides. "Why don't you get on back to Rafe and tell him his little plan fell through? You and I don't need to talk. All we need to do is forget we ever knew each other."

"Right," she spit out, then whirled and started away. She saw Rafe waiting up the road. All alone, he looked lost and desolate standing there, his hands shoved deep into his pockets, his shoulders hunched. Surprised, Thawn stopped dead in her tracks.

But she hardly had time to take in the picture when a hand caught her arm. "Thawn." Mark was beside her once again. "Listen, I'm sorry. I didn't mean to bark at you that way."

He was trying. It was only fair that she make the same effort. "I'm sorry too," she said, swallowing hard and meeting his blue eyes.

"Let's start over again," Mark said lightly, slipping an arm around her shoulders and drawing her back to the open place where they'd been talking before. She glanced back over her shoulder to where Rafe had been standing, but he was gone.

Mark was still talking. "I had to express some of my anger. But that's over now. Instead of telling you how you've ruined my life, I should have been telling you how you saved it."

She gazed up at him, openmouthed, as he nodded. "I was heading down a dangerous road and I couldn't see it for myself. I was ready to pay any price for what I wanted. When the article came out, everything stopped cold. I had a good long time to think, to take stock, to reevaluate my goals and methods."

He ran a careless hand through his blond curls. "Things have really changed for me now. I know I can make it on my own talent and hard work. And who knows? If it hadn't been for you, I might never have discovered that."

They looked into each other's eyes for a long moment. Then Thawn tried a tentative smile. "Oh, Mark." She reached out to take his hand. "I never wanted anyone to write anything about you. I was devastated by what happened, and I turned to the wrong person to sob my heart out to. If I'd dreamed what she would do with it..."

Suddenly it was like talking to the old Mark, only better. They could laugh again, and that was nice. But she didn't love him anymore. The emotion she'd once felt had been totally obscured by what she felt for Rafe.

"He's crazy about you, you know," Mark said, as though reading her mind. "When he called me last night to tell me he was bringing you up here, he told me he was going to marry you." He grinned. "Believe it or not, I told him he couldn't have made a better choice."

Marry her. Thawn's heart began to thump at the words. Could he really have said that? Why would Mark mention it if it wasn't true?

Rafe had offered to marry her the day before. He'd used it to tease her today. But she'd never really believed in his intention. She'd taken it as a ploy to avert a breakup when he wasn't ready for one. But if he was telling other people . . .

As soon as she could, Thawn excused herself from the conversation. It was nice to know that she and Mark were no longer enemies, but her first priority was the man she had seen standing all alone a few minutes before. Suddenly she wanted to find him very badly.

People were milling everywhere, some wearing costumes for some sort of party scene, others dressed like technicians. She pushed her way past them, searching for the face she loved.

They were about to film a scene. Directors were hurrying people into place and yelling for everyone to be quiet. Thawn stopped a moment to watch as the lights and cameras, like giant insects, focused on the two people playing the scene.

"Quiet on the set!"

"Rolling!"

"Take six."

"Action!"

Thawn was impressed by the professionalism. Now that she understood more about what went into making a film, she saw what part each onlooker played in the event. So many people, so much equipment, so very much work to get each scene shot. She shook her head, marveling. It really was a fascinating way to make a living.

"Thawn Carlton?"

She turned toward the voice and smiled expectantly at the short, dark-eyed woman before her. Of middle years, she had the sharp, predatory look of a carnivorous bird.

"I thought that was you." The woman grinned companionably, as though the two of them were old friends. "How have you been, dear?"

Thawn endured the brush of the woman's lips against her cheek, sure she'd never seen her before in her life.

"Where have you been hiding yourself? I'm so glad we're going to have a chance to get to know each other after all."

At least the woman admitted she wasn't the long-lost friend she had first pretended to be.

"I'm afraid I don't know who you are," Thawn said bluntly. Something about this woman told her that being direct was the only way to handle the situation.

"Don't you?" The woman pouted. "Here's my card."

She handed Thawn a pale blue rectangle on which was embossed: Sally Creaston, Show Business Editor, *Star Spy*. Thawn looked up quickly. Here was another Jacqui Blatts, another scandal hound, an employee of a rival paper.

"Thanks," said Thawn crisply, "but no thanks." She handed the card calmly back to the woman and turned to leave.

"Wait a minute, honey. I think you'll be interested in this."

With a gilt pen she quickly dashed off a message on the card and tucked it into the pocket of Thawn's dark corduroy slacks. "That's how much I could get for you on an exclusive about Rafe Armstrong," she hissed *"Star Spy* will pay, honey. Just give me a chance to..."

Thawn was backing away, her hands spread as though

to keep from touching poison. "Stay away from me," she said hoarsely. "Don't even speak to me again. Ever."

Turning, she ran down the dirt road, back toward the trees, gripped by a strange, overwhelming compulsion to find Rafe. She had to touch him, to make sure he was real.

Finally she saw him, still surrounded by people. Her heart lurched as she realized that the crowd around him consisted almost exclusively of beautiful women. He was smiling in answer to some comment a stunning brunet had made into his ear. At that moment he caught sight of Thawn, and the smile on his face became an expression that tore at her heart.

He loved her. Could it really be true? In that moment she knew she would stay with him for as long as he wanted her. Whether the love she saw was for the moment, for the week, or for a lifetime, she would stay as long as it lasted.

She watched him come toward her, his eyes full of emotion, and she held out her hands to him. He took her in his arms and held her close.

"Is it all right?" he whispered.

"Yes," she answered happily.

"Good." He released her. "Then let's get out of here."

"On with the honeymoon?" she teased.

"Absolutely." He led her back to where the car was parked, and soon they were roaring up the highway again.

She knew he was curious about what had happened between her and Mark, but she couldn't tell him about it yet. Soon, but not just now. She settled back in her seat and reached out to ruffle the hair at his collar line.

"Now will you tell me where we're going?"

CHAPTER TWELVE

RAFE SENT THAWN a long sideways look. "I hope you're not expecting some swank resort motel with chandeliers and maid service," he warned.

She pretended indignation. "Of course I am. This is a honeymoon, isn't it?"

He moved uncomfortably in the driver's seat. "This is a different sort of honeymoon," he said evasively. "You like different things, don't you?"

She cocked an eyebrow. "Only if they're nice. Is this nice?"

He shrugged. "It's a cabin in the woods," he admitted.

She thought that over for a moment. "A *nice* cabin in the woods?"

He smiled. "You're the nature girl. You should be able to rough it for a few days."

"A few days! I have to get back to work."

He shook his head. "Tom promised to fix that for you. Don't give it another thought."

"Just what do you have in mind?"

His long, expressive sigh gave ample evidence of what his plans included. "This is the last chance we'll have to spend time together," he told her. "By the end of the week, I'll be leaving for Wyoming to begin full-time work on the Western. I won't have much time to go off on honeymoons then."

Thawn turned and watched the dark tree trunks whiz by the window. So he was leaving after all. At least he was putting off his departure for a few days so that they could have some time together before he left.

Neither of them spoke for a long while. Thawn watched as the countryside changed from forested mountains to rolling hills covered with cattle, from farmland to rugged headlands.

"Here we are," Rafe finally announced.

Suddenly the car was plunging down a very steep road that had been cut into the face of the cliff. They seemed to be hurtling toward the sea.

"Rafe!" Thawn cried, planting her feet firmly against the floorboard and holding on tightly.

"Don't worry," he answered calmly as he slowed the car to make a sudden turn. "You've got to learn to love these steep descents if you want to build your house on a cliff overlooking the surf."

He parked behind a wooden structure hidden by a stand of huge ponderosa pine. Thawn wasn't sure her legs would hold her up after the harrowing trip down the mountain, but when she got out of the car, she found them strong enough, if shaky.

"Here's our cabin."

She looked up and gasped. Instead of the rustic building she'd been expecting, she saw a stunning modern home of tinted glass and redwood that was cantilevered out over the sea.

Rafe put an arm around her shoulders as they walked toward the house. "How do you like it, nature girl?" he asked softly.

"Cabin in the woods?" she reminded him mockingly. "You didn't get this through State Park Reservations. Whose place is this?"

"A friend of mine. A director I know." He produced a key and opened the door to the entryway. "I told him I needed a hideaway for a few days, and he offered us unlimited use."

The interior was as impressive as the exterior, with tan and white Peruvian rugs on polished hardwood floors, a tremendous natural granite fireplace, and Mayan murals and Aztec wall hangings.

The house looked out onto the sea. Standing at the dark glass windows that formed the forward wall, all Thawn could see below was the white foam of crashing surf as it pounded the jagged rocks.

"I hope we've got good moorings," she murmured, looking down into the chilly ocean. "I'd hate to wake up with my bed floating in that water."

"Don't worry." Rafe pulled her close and kissed her gently. "We'll just set sail for Hawaii and continue our honeymoon there."

"We won't have time for Hawaii," she replied, trying to keep her voice light as he left her embrace to pace around the room. "After all, you'll be starting on the Western. You'll have to get back to all your Hollywood cronies."

He stopped at her words and turned toward her. She could feel his gaze on her. She ran her fingers across the warm, well-polished wood of the guardrail in front of the window and waited.

"You really don't feel comfortable with those people,

do you, Thawn?" he asked quietly. "I never realized that before, but I saw it right away at the set. You didn't like being there."

Her fingers tightened on the wood, and she closed her eyes. He'd finally realized that she wouldn't fit in. He knew now how impossible it was for them ever to have a lasting relationship. His life was his work. It was a life she could never share.

There was no point in trying to pretend. "No," she admitted, her voice surprisingly strong, "I didn't particularly like it." She turned to face him. "I don't like the pushing and shoving for attention. I don't like the constant feeling that everyone is putting himself on the auction block, up for sale to the highest bidder." She shrugged. "That was one of the reasons Mark and I split up."

. There. It was all out in the open. He couldn't ignore the truth any longer.

"It's too bad," Rafe said softly. "Really too bad." He turned again. "I'm going out to the car to get the bags."

Thawn stayed where she was, tears stinging her eyes. But she wouldn't cry. She'd known from the beginning how it would end. Why not make the best of this moment? It was probably all she had left.

By the time Rafe returned, she'd managed to put a smile back on her face. "You get full suitcases, but what am I supposed to do for clothes?" she complained good-naturedly.

He cocked a dark eyebrow at her. "You wouldn't consider going nude?"

She laughed. "No, I would not. Not with this stiff wind blowing off the Pacific."

He dropped the bags and came over to take her face in his hands. "We could stay inside," he murmured,

nibbling at one earlobe, then the other. "We could keep the windows closed."

She circled him with her arms, holding him loosely. "Not on your life," she answered pleasantly but firmly.

"Then it's a good thing I brought you a whole suitcase full of clothes." He grinned at her startled reaction. "I had Carly pack up things you'd left at the trailer. She added items of her own that you'd be missing."

"You're wonderful!" She hugged him. "Does this little cabin in the woods have running water? I'd love to take a bath."

Rafe started a blaze in the fireplace while she scrubbed away the day's dirt. She pulled back on her tight-fitting corduroy pants and a clean silky blue blouse before re-joining him.

She found him staring moodily out to sea, just as she'd been doing a short time ago. Stopping for a moment before he could hear her approach, she watched him.

How she loved the long, lanky grace of him, the suppressed energy, the humor that so often lit his gray eyes. He was dressed in jeans and a dark sweater over a yellow cotton shirt that set off his dark tan and crisp, dark brown hair in a way that looked clean and compelling.

As she watched, he lowered his head and rubbed his hands across his face as though he was very tired. When he raised his head again, he caught sight of her, and for just a moment they stared at one another without smiling.

What was he thinking, Thawn wondered. She walked slowly toward him, and he reached out to touch her cheek.

"I've just had a thought," he said lightly. "You showed me your blackberries and your cave. I know a place here that's magic too."

She tried to smile in response. "Really? Where is it?"

"Come on," he told her, becoming excited. "I'll show you. It's only a short hike from here."

The sun was hanging low in the sky, but it was still strong enough to warm their backs as they made their way up the incline.

"We'll cut in here through these redwoods," he told her, steering her into a dark, forested patch of wilderness.

"You've visited here before, haven't you?" she asked idly as they climbed, then slid down a rocky incline, then climbed again.

"The house? Sure. Jerry's a good friend. I've been to some of his holiday weekends out here, and he's let me use his place before when he wasn't going to be coming out." He helped her up a jagged rock, then led her through a stand of cypress. "Just a little farther," he assured her. "We're almost there."

She knew immediately when they arrived at the location. The place was perfect, a fitting reward for the hike. Water fell like diamond spears from a small waterfall in the rock wall above their heads. Pale green ferns grew from the black cliff face. The stream tumbled noisily as it started its journey down to the sea.

A sudden hush had filled the air as they entered the little grotto, which was enclosed all around by redwoods and California laurel. Thawn felt as if there should be organ music playing, as though no one should speak above a whisper.

Rafe's arms slipped around her from behind. "How do you think this stacks up against your special places?" he asked.

She smiled at him over her shoulder. "At the head of the list. I love this place, Rafe. There's a special stillness here. I feel as though I should be praying."

He nuzzled into the hollow of her shoulder. "That's the way I feel about it, too. That's why I brought you here—to give you a present."

"A present?"

He released her and reached into the pocket of his slacks. "Here." He offered the little box awkwardly, as though he was suddenly uncomfortable. "This is for you."

She took the box and opened it. Inside, on a bed of white cotton, lay a small sea otter carved out of jade. The style was much like that of bone carvings done by the Alaskan Indians, and Thawn gasped at its beauty.

"Is this the piece of jade you found that day you were diving off your property?" she asked, delighted.

He nodded. "The piece you handed back to me so angrily. I heard about an artist in Cambria who does this sort of thing. I took a look at his work and decided I wanted him to do it for you."

She cradled the lovely little animal in the palm of her hand. "It's beautiful." Her voice was choked, and tears filled her eyes. Avoiding Rafe's scrutiny, she put the carving back into the box and tried to stuff it into the pocket of her pants. Something fell out as she did so— a blue rectangle; Sally Creaston's card.

Rafe bent and picked up the card. As Thawn watched, time seemed to slow down so that she could see each movement in slow motion—his strong fingers against the dark green moss as he touched the card; the slow, inexorable path of the card as it came up to where he could begin to read it; his frown as the message written on the back became clear to him.

She closed her eyes and turned away. She knew what he would think when he saw whose card it was and noted the payment price written on the back. Did she really have to defend herself all over again? Maybe the best

thing would be to have an argument now that would be so bad, so overwhelming, they would know it was over between them. Perhaps that would be better than a long drawn-out period of indecision and separation.

She knew what Rafe was thinking. This suspicion would always be there. She didn't want to wait around to hear the accusations.

She began to follow the stream toward the waterfall. The silver liquid looked cool and refreshing. She wanted to stand under its shower and let the water cleanse away her heartache.

"They never give up, do they?"

Something in Rafe's voice stopped her. Slowly she turned and looked back.

He was crushing the card in his hand, turning it into a tiny blue ball of paper.

"I swear if a helicopter came over right now, I'd expect to see Jacqui Blatts, or this harpie, or another one of them with a camera, snapping away."

His mouth held the ghost of a smile. Could that really be? He seemed to be thinking with reluctant affection about the foibles of these people rather than with the hatred and bitterness she'd expected.

He walked toward her as he stuffed the little paper ball into his pocket. "I'm sorry. I guess you'll have to put up with that sort of thing from now on."

He stopped a few feet from her. She stared up at him, too surprised to speak. There was no blame in his eyes, only a raw vulnerability that twisted her heart.

"What can I offer you, Thawn?" His voice was husky with emotion. "What can I do to convince you to love me?"

Her hands went to her face. She wasn't sure if she was hearing him quite right.

"I know you think my love for you isn't deep enough. You don't trust it." His gaze moved hungrily over the planes of her face. "I know you hate the sort of life I lead. The people..." He reached for her. "What can I do to make you love me?" he whispered.

"Oh, Rafe..."

"I need you so much, my lovely lady." He began dropping short burning kisses on her eyes, her cheeks, her lips. "Please say you'll stay with me."

His voice was strangely hoarse, as though the effort to say these words was contorting it. All at once she knew she couldn't leave him, that she would hold on to what they had, for as long as she could, no matter what the future held.

"I will. Oh, Rafe, I'll stay as long as you want me to."

His fingers tightened and he held her face away, glaring down at her. "Can't you get it through your skull this is for keeps?" he growled. "What I feel for you isn't temporary. I want to marry you. And I've never said that to another woman. Never."

He pulled her against him and held her tight, rocking with her to the rhythm of the gurling stream. "I knew you were different from the first time I saw you. The longer I stayed, the more you trapped me, nature girl. I'll never be free again."

Thawn pulled back and stared into his eyes. He'd never put it quite so plainly before. He really did want to marry her. Suddenly she found herself laughing. "Is that a complaint or a compliment?" she said with a chortle. She was happier than she'd ever been. Rafe's face was warm where she touched it, and she rubbed her cheek lightly against his.

"Neither." He hugged her tightly. "It's a statement of

fact. I'll never be free again, no matter what you decide to do. I'll never feel this way with anyone else."

She closed her eyes and listened to his heartbeat. It was steady, strong, something to rely on.

"Well?" He pulled roughly away and gazed at her, the questions still burning in his eyes. "What are you going to do?"

She looked up at him, her lips parted hesitantly. "Marry you?" she whispered. That was what he meant, wasn't it?

"No, damn it," he growled. "I don't want to hear that as a question. I want to hear you shout it like you mean it!"

Her grin answered his. "I'm going to marry you!" she cried.

"All right!"

As he lowered his dark head to kiss her, she felt laughter bubbling up and heard it echo in him. But the laughter soon died as his lips moved over hers. There was a fire burning between them now, and they both felt it and knew it would be difficult to quench.

"Thawn, darling," he breathed upon her skin as his mouth left hers to explore the pulse that throbbed behind her ear. "You've tortured me for so long!"

She sighed and pressed herself against him, luxuriating in the hardness of his long body. "I'm sorry," she murmured. "I was so afraid..."

His tongue was making lazy circles along the hairline at her temple. A lovely, languid feeling was overtaking her. She closed her eyes and arched her neck, presenting it for more of his golden touch.

"Don't ever be afraid with me, darling." His breath stirred the tiny hairs along her skin and sent the blood surging through her veins. "I'm putty in your hands. You can do what you want with me."

As if that were a cue, she found herself pulling at his shirt, loosening it and slipping her hands in underneath to capture the heat of his chest. He groaned as her fingers gently tickled his crisp hair.

"You can especially do that," he muttered, reaching down to pull his sweater and shirt off, giving her free access. She splayed her fingers across his chest, marveling at how beautiful flesh could be.

"And now it's my turn," he whispered as he deftly tugged free the fastenings of her silky blouse. Instinctively she tried to pull the cloth back against her breasts, but he tore it firmly free, then dispensed with her lacy bra.

The breeze was cool on her skin and her nipples tightened in the evening air, but she didn't try to cover herself. She could trust him now. She was sure of it.

They lay back in a bed of ferns. Sunlight fell through the trees in dappled spots of color on their naked skin. Spray from the water hitting the rocks beside them cooled the air they breathed. Birds chattered in the treetops, and the gurgling stream made its own music in the background.

Rafe slowly explored Thawn's body, taking his time, running his fingers across the slope of her breast, circling the dip of her navel, lightly teasing the tiny hairs that covered her thighs.

She leaned back lazily, watching him with eyes half-closed, holding back the involuntary moans that rose in her at his touch. Finally she became impatient and arched up at his hand, reaching to pull him against her.

"Do you want me, Thawn?" he asked huskily. "Tell me."

"I want you," she groaned obediently. "I want you now."

"Oh no, nature girl." He laughed softly as he evaded

her attempt to draw him closer. His fingers nipped at the tips of her breasts, but he wouldn't let her feel his body hard against her. "We have to take this slowly. We want to do it naturally."

She opened her eyes and stared at him, slightly confused. "What? What's natural about slow?" she demanded foggily.

He grinned. "You've heard the song. 'Love comes slow, can't be rushed, you've got to hold on . . .'"

She knew he was teasing her, and she didn't stop to evaluate her next move. He'd built the fire that burned in her and only he could deal with it now. She twisted quickly, pouncing on him so that he fell back against the ferns and she was on top. With her palms pressing his shoulders down, she moved against him, twining her legs with his, stretching up so that she could look down into his face.

"Now tell me about how love comes that slow," she murmured, glorying in the instant response in his eyes. "Tell me about how we just have to hold on."

He growled and covered her hips with his hands, pulling her to him, and he reversed positions again, and the wait was over.

As they came together, she cried out his name and he groaned out his love for her, urging her on until they found the center of the tempest together and rode it to exhaustion.

Afterward they lay so still for so long that Thawn began to wonder if they'd lost all power of movement. It felt so wonderful to be with Rafe, to feel his warmth on her skin, his breath in her hair.

"You're still going to marry me, aren't you?" His voice was a rough intrusion into her dreamlike state.

"Of course." She twisted around so that she could see

into his eyes. "I'm going to do everything I can to make you happy." She came up on her elbows. "Rafe, about . . . the movie-making business. You said you could tell I didn't feel comfortable with those people. And you were right. But I can learn. With you to help me, I'll find a way."

He lifted a lazy hand to push back her hair as it fell down over her face in a golden curtain. "It may not be as difficult as you think," he said slowly.

"You don't think I'll distract you?" she asked hesitantly, thinking of what Harry had said. "You don't think I'll keep you from making a total effort?"

He laughed softly. "I'm becoming a new man, Thawn. I'm learning all about moderation. I've been obsessed at times, but that was when I was working my way up, when I was unsure of my direction. I know what I'm doing now. I can relax and live a more normal life." He smiled at her. "Besides, I've come up with some of my best ideas this summer while spending lazy time with you. When we go back home, I'll show you some of the plans I've set up for future projects."

"I'd like that." She grinned back at him. "Who knows? Maybe I could give you some ideas myself."

He nodded seriously. "You already have. Talking with you helped me develop a theme of man's impact on the changing landscape for the Western." He paused, then went on almost apologetically, "I'm going to be involved in my Western epic from start to finish. And for that I want you with me." He shifted his weight and moved to join her in a half-sitting position. "But after that's finished, I'm thinking of making a few changes."

She frowned. "Rafe, you mustn't change the work you love because of me!"

He stilled her protest with a finger on her lips. "I'm

not. Believe me, this is something I've been thinking about for a long time." His smile was tender. "I've always enjoyed the conceptual work a lot more than the line production, coming up with ideas rather than implementing them. And that's what I'll be doing from now on—blocking out concepts, writing scripts. But the location production will be done by collaborators. Jeff Corwin will be doing some things with me. And I hope Mark will be working with me on some adventure films I'm thinking about."

Thawn gazed at him, fascinated. "You mean you won't be on the set while they're shooting?"

He nodded. "I'll be in our house on the coast, working on new ideas."

She opened her mouth, shut it, then opened it again. "But that means . . ."

"That means we won't have to live in Hollywood. That means you can keep your job. That means we won't have long separations while I'm off on location somewhere."

Her heart swelled with love for him. "Oh, Rafe. It'll be perfect!"

"Perfect." He kissed the tip of her nose.

She caught hold of him and forced his mouth down to meet hers. "Wow," he breathed when she let him go. "You nature people never get enough of that stuff, do you?"

"Not when it's such quality stuff," she teased, feeling wicked.

He leaned back, sighing with contentment, and she smiled. "So you really are going to do more work with Mark," she murmured speculatively. "That was why you wanted us to make up."

"Yes." He hesitated, then added, "That and more."

His eyes held hers and she searched them, wondering at the shadows there. "I had to be sure it was really over between you."

She hadn't considered that possibility. "Oh, Rafe..."

"You don't know what it cost me to watch you with him today," he said hoarsely. "When he put his arm around you..."

"You thought we might renew what we had?" It seemed an incredible idea to her, but she could see how he had viewed it. "Never. Don't you know how much I love you?"

His head snapped around. "What did you say?" he demanded.

She looked at him, puzzled. "I love you," she said softly.

Were his eyes misting, or was it the hazy evening light filtering through the trees?

"Thawn," he rasped, his voice thick with emotion, "that's the first time you've said 'I love you.'"

How could that be? She'd been thinking it for so long. With tears in her eyes, she reached for him. "I promise you, darling," she whispered against his chest, "it won't be the last."

_____ 06540-4 **FROM THE TORRID PAST #49** Ann Cristy
_____ 06544-7 **RECKLESS LONGING #50** Daisy Logan
_____ 05851-3 **LOVE'S MASQUERADE #51** Lillian Marsh
_____ 06148-4 **THE STEELE HEART #52** Jocelyn Day
_____ 06422-X **UNTAMED DESIRE #53** Beth Brookes
_____ 06651-6 **VENUS RISING #54** Michelle Roland
_____ 06595-1 **SWEET VICTORY #55** Jena Hunt
_____ 06575-7 **TOO NEAR THE SUN #56** Aimée Duvall
_____ 05625-1 **MOURNING BRIDE #57** Lucia Curzon
_____ 06411-4 **THE GOLDEN TOUCH #58** Robin James
_____ 06596-X **EMBRACED BY DESTINY #59** Simone Hadary
_____ 06660-5 **TORN ASUNDER #60** Ann Cristy
_____ 06573-0 **MIRAGE #61** Margie Michaels
_____ 06650-8 **ON WINGS OF MAGIC #62** Susanna Collins
_____ 05816-5 **DOUBLE DECEPTION #63** Amanda Troy
_____ 06675-3 **APOLLO'S DREAM #64** Claire Evans
_____ 06680-X **THE ROGUE'S LADY #69** Anne Devon
_____ 06689-3 **SWEETER THAN WINE #78** Jena Hunt
_____ 06690-7 **SAVAGE EDEN #79** Diane Crawford
_____ 06692-3 **THE WAYWARD WIDOW #81** Anne Mayfield
_____ 06693-1 **TARNISHED RAINBOW #82** Jocelyn Day
_____ 06694-X **STARLIT SEDUCTION #83** Anne Reed
_____ 06695-8 **LOVER IN BLUE #84** Aimée Duvall

All of the above titles are $1.75 per copy

_____ 06696-6 THE FAMILIAR TOUCH #85 Lynn Lawrence

_____ 06697-4 TWILIGHT EMBRACE #86 Jennifer Rose

_____ 06698-2 QUEEN OF HEARTS #87 Lucia Curzon

_____ 06850-0 PASSION'S SONG #88 Johanna Phillips

_____ 06851-9 A MAN'S PERSUASION #89 Katherine Granger

_____ 06852-7 FORBIDDEN RAPTURE #90 Kate Nevins

_____ 06853-5 THIS WILD HEART #91 Margarett McKean

_____ 06854-3 SPLENDID SAVAGE #92 Zandra Colt

_____ 06855-1 THE EARL'S FANCY #93 Charlotte Hines

_____ 06858-6 BREATHLESS DAWN #94 Susanna Collins

_____ 06859-4 SWEET SURRENDER #95 Diana Mars

_____ 06860-8 GUARDED MOMENTS #96 Lynn Fairfax

_____ 06861-6 ECSTASY RECLAIMED #97 Brandy LaRue

_____ 06862-4 THE WIND'S EMBRACE #98 Melinda Harris

_____ 06863-2 THE FORGOTTEN BRIDE #99 Lillian Marsh

_____ 06864-0 A PROMISE TO CHERISH #100 LaVyrle Spencer

_____ 06865-9 GENTLE AWAKENING #101 Marianne Cole

_____ 06866-7 BELOVED STRANGER #102 Michelle Roland

_____ 06867-5 ENTHRALLED #103 Ann Cristy

_____ 06869-1 DEFIANT MISTRESS #105 Anne Devon

_____ 06870-5 RELENTLESS DESIRE #106 Sandra Brown

_____ 06871-3 SCENES FROM THE HEART #107 Marie Charles

_____ 06872-1 SPRING FEVER #108 Simone Hadary

_____ 06873-X IN THE ARMS OF A STRANGER #109 Deborah Joyce

_____ 06874-8 TAKEN BY STORM #110 Kay Robbins

_____ 06899-3 THE ARDENT PROTECTOR #111 Amanda Kent

_____ 07200-1 A LASTING TREASURE #112 Cally Hughes $1.95

All of the above titles are $1.75 per copy except where noted

---

____ 07201-X **RESTLESS TIDES #113** Kelly Adams $1.95
____ 07202-8 **MOONLIGHT PERSUASION #114** Sharon Stone $1.95
____ 07203-6 **COME WINTER'S END #115** Claire Evans $1.95
____ 07204-4 **LET PASSION SOAR #116** Sherry Carr $1.95
____ 07205-2 **LONDON FROLIC #117** Josephine Janes $1.95
____ 07206-0 **IMPRISONED HEART #118** Jasmine Craig $1.95
____ 07207-9 **THE MAN FROM TENNESSEE #119** Jeanne Grant $1.95
____ 07208-7 **LAUGH WITH ME, LOVE WITH ME #120** Lee Damon $1.95
____ 07209-5 **PLAY IT BY HEART #121** Vanessa Valcour $1.95
____ 07210-9 **SWEET ABANDON #122** Diana Mars $1.95
____ 07211-7 **THE DASHING GUARDIAN #123** Lucia Curzon $1.95
____ 07212-5 **SONG FOR A LIFETIME #124** Mary Haskell $1.95
____ 07213-3 **HIDDEN DREAMS #125** Johanna Phillips $1.95
____ 07214-1 **LONGING UNVEILED #126** Meredith Kingston $1.95
____ 07215-X **JADE TIDE #127** Jena Hunt $1.95
____ 07216-8 **THE MARRYING KIND #128** Jocelyn Day $1.95
____ 07217-6 **CONQUERING EMBRACE #129** Ariel Tierney $1.95

WHAT READERS SAY ABOUT
SECOND CHANCE AT LOVE BOOKS

"Your books are the greatest!"
—*M. N., Carteret, New Jersey**

"I have been reading romance novels for quite some time, but the SECOND CHANCE AT LOVE books are the most enjoyable."
—*P. R., Vicksburg, Mississippi**

"I enjoy SECOND CHANCE [AT LOVE] more than any books that I have read and I do read a lot."
—*J. R., Gretna, Louisiana**

"I really think your books are exceptional . . . I read Harlequin and Silhouette and although I still like them, I'll buy your books over theirs. SECOND CHANCE [AT LOVE] is more interesting and holds your attention and imagination with a better story line . . ."
—*J. W., Flagstaff, Arizona**

"I've read many romances, but yours take the 'cake'!"
—*D. H., Bloomsburg, Pennsylvania**

"Have waited ten years for *good* romance books. Now I have them."
—*M. P., Jacksonville, Florida**

*Names and addresses available upon request